THE STAGE DOOR

"When he talked of my art he really seemed inspired."

THE
STAGE DOOR

BY
CHARLES BELMONT DAVIS

ILLUSTRATED

Short Story Index Reprint Series

BOOKS FOR LIBRARIES PRESS
FREEPORT, NEW YORK

First Published 1908
Reprinted 1970

STANDARD BOOK NUMBER:
8369-3526-8

LIBRARY OF CONGRESS CATALOG CARD NUMBER:
74-122693

PRINTED IN THE UNITED STATES OF AMERICA

To

MY MOTHER

CONTENTS

ILLUSTRATIONS

EVERYMAN'S RIDDLE

EVERYMAN'S RIDDLE

OURS was the second train to arrive after the accident, and while the towering mass of wreckage had remained untouched, most of the human suffering had been fairly well put under cover. The killed had either been carried into the section house or covered with blankets, and the doctors who had arrived a short time before us were looking after the more seriously injured in one of the coaches of their special.

It was about five o'clock when our train slowed up and the brakeman ran down the aisle of the smoking-car and with his big fist broke in the glass door of the tool-case. Naturally when he jumped off the platform we followed him, and away ahead of us we could see the two engines smashed and bent, but erect and holding each other up like two great, brutal, fighting animals standing on their

3

hind legs, too tired to strike out and finish the battle. The day coaches and the sleeping-cars were piled about like a lot of children's blocks in a nursery. It was early in June, and the sky was quite cloudless and a deep blue, and the turf was a marshy green and yielding; the air was full of the smell of wild flowers and little birds were hopping about and chirping all over the place. It was a day that would suggest anything else in the world before death, and there it was —death, and worse than death on every side of us.

I looked about for a while in the hope of helping some one, but we were too late to be of any real service; it was a case for the doctors, in most instances, and how can a stranger comfort a man who has just seen his wife and children mangled out of recognition and wiped out of his life forever? Of course, there were some of them that were hysterical to the point of danger, and there were others that sat about their dead, dry-eyed and looking out across the fields as if the setting of the sun was the only thing that was of any real interest to them in the world. I picked my way across a stream that ran by the road-bed and climbed up a little hill overlooking the wreck.

The hill was thick with pine-trees and the ground, slippery with brown needles, was strewn with pieces of painted wood from the cars and glistening, twisted bits of machinery from the two engines. There were a good many odd pieces of men's and women's clothing, too, lying about, and quite a number of broken hats and some pieces of trunks and suit-cases. Half-way up the hill a little group of passen-gers had gathered about a young man who was sit-ting on the ground, his back against a pine-tree. He had evidently been placed there until the doctors could carry him away on one of their improvised stretchers. The little circle who stood about him must have annoyed him, for as I approached I saw him half raise his arm and motion them away. It was a feeble effort at best, but I suppose they knew what he meant, for the party suddenly broke up into couples and wandered back to the wreck. At the moment I was standing perhaps twenty feet away and a little back of him, so he probably believed that he was quite alone. He was a young man, perhaps twenty-eight or thirty—neither good nor bad look-ing, I should think, but it was difficult to tell exactly, as his face was gray as putty and all screwed up with the pain. He was smooth-shaven and he had red hair and was dressed as a man would who was in good circumstances. When the circle about him had broken up and the men had started down the hill, I noticed that a look of great relief seemed to come into his face. His head still resting against the tree, he looked up for a moment through the straight branches of the pines to the patches of blue sky above. I could see his face more clearly then, and during that moment I am sure that the pain had left him, that his mind was clear, and that he had asked his last favor on this earth. For a moment he closed his eyes, and when he opened them again it was evident that he saw the little group of men who were coming toward him with the stretcher. And then I saw him raise his arm with great difficulty and take from the inside pocket of his coat a folded piece of a newspaper. This he spread out upon his knees, but after one brief glance he crumpled it in both hands and threw it as far away from him as his feeble strength allowed.

They carried him away down the little hill over

the soft carpet of pine-needles, glowing like copper in the broad shafts of the evening sun. As they reached the creek I saw the arm of the young man, which had been resting over his eyes, suddenly fall to his side. For a moment the little procession halted; one of the physicians knelt at the side of the litter and looked searchingly into the face of the young man. Then the doctor pulled himself to his feet again and nodded in the direction of the section house, and they carried him on very slowly and very silently, with their hats in their hands. As I started down the hill I saw the crumpled piece of paper which the young man had thrown away lying but a few feet from me. For a moment I hesitated, and then I went over to where it lay and picked it up. It was half a page torn from the Saturday illustrated supplement of a New York evening paper. At the first glance it looked dull enough, but I felt sure that somewhere it contained at least a minor story in the life of the young man; so I carefully folded the torn, crumpled sheet and put it away in my pocket. Then I walked down to the section house where the young man had already been identified by some letters and his visiting-cards. His name was Hugh Musgrove and the address given was "Editorial Rooms—*The Evening* ——, New York."

It was some hours later, when our train had started on a long circuitous route to New York, that ·I again looked at the torn piece of newspaper that Musgrove had thrown away just previous to his death. On one side there was a description of a recent flood in the Far West and some illustrations showing the damage it had done; the other side was part of the dramatic department of the paper and the letter press was devoted to a description of several theatrical attractions which were to open in New York the following Monday. In addition to the letter press there were three pictures—all of women. The centre and largest picture of the three was a big, handsome woman, dressed in the robes of Brunhilde. The caption under the picture read—"Madame Carlotta Helma, who gives her farewell song recital Thursday afternoon at Carnegie Hall." On the right side of this there was a picture of a very young woman with a slight girlish figure and a face remarkable for a wonderful purity and sweetness of

8

expression. She was dressed in a very simple evening dress and was posed as if about to begin playing the violin. Under this picture was the line, "Miss Agnes Beach, who makes her *début* Wednesday night with the Philharmonic Society orchestra at Chickering Hall." The third picture was that of a young woman, remarkable at least for her figure and a wealth of hair, which may or may not have been a wig. She had big eyes, clean-cut features, and although she was undoubtedly heavily made up when the original photograph had been taken, her beauty was easily evident. The caption read: "Miss Deane Kimball, in the Cockatoo chorus of 'The Belle and the Bandit,' which opens Monday night at the Casino."

Perhaps it was from mere curiosity, or perhaps there was an underlying hope of doing a kindly act in telling one of the three women the last incident in the life of Musgrove, but whatever the motive, when I returned to New York, I wrote a letter to each of the three. The addresses of Madame Helma and Miss Beach I learned through a musical agency. The letter to Miss Kimball I mailed to the Casino. This is what I wrote in each letter:

DEAR MADAM: Following the recent terrible railroad accident at Mill's Crossing, it was my misfortune to be present at the death of a young man whom, I believe, you numbered among your friends. As it is purely a private matter, I am tempted to ask you to permit me to call on you personally, rather than to write you concerning the incident. Believe me,

Yours truly, etc.

For several days after the accident I carefully read the newspapers to obtain, if possible, some information concerning Hugh Musgrove. In the revised lists of the dead he was referred to as either the assistant musical, or assistant dramatic, critic of *The Evening* ———, or merely as a journalist. Not a word about his home or his family, and the last I saw about him in the papers was a paragraph to the effect that he had been buried from an Eighth Avenue undertaker's shop.

Within forty-eight hours after I had mailed my letters I received an answer from each of the three women. Madame Helma asked me to call the following evening at half past six o'clock at the Cambridge Hotel; Miss Beach, who answered me through her father, said that she could see me any evening after eight o'clock at her home on Clinton Place; Miss Kimball sent me as her address The Barclay, on West Forty-third Street, and said that she could usually be found at home between five and seven-thirty in the evening. None of them mentioned Musgrove's name, but that did not surprise me, as I had refrained from writing it myself, and in a wreck of such proportions as the one at Mill's Crossing, it was possible for almost every one to have numbered one or more friends in the list of the killed.

With the torn piece of newspaper in my coat pocket I presented myself the next evening at the Cambridge and was shown to Madame Helma's apartment. Of the woman I knew but little beyond the fact that she was born in America and that she was recognized as one of the greatest dramatic sopranos in the world. In a vague way I rather imagined I had heard that she had been married to an Austrian officer of title. I did not for a moment believe that she was the one of the three women who had interested the ill-fated Musgrove, but it was part of my general plan to call on all three of them, and

the appointment which she had made for me was the
first to find me at leisure. Madame occupied a suite
on the third floor of the hotel at the corner overlooking
Fifth Avenue. Her Austrian husband, with a small,
tawny pointed mustache and a tawny pointed beard,
met me at the door and showed me with much manner into the drawing-room. For a few moments we
chatted on purely impersonal subjects, looked at
large, fiercely autographed photographs of other
opera singers which stood about on the mantel-shelf
and piano, and then the portières opened and Madame Helma herself appeared. She was a very big,
fine-looking woman, and in the little *salon* and by the
side of her husband, she really appeared quite heroic
in size. She was evidently on her way to dinner, and
her dress and opera-cloak as well as her jewels were
really regal. Her manner to me, might be described,
in a general way, as gracious, but it was the gra-
ciousness of the truly condescending and like the
few other opera singers I have known, her belief in
herself was so great that she appeared as two women
—the great artist standing quite apart, the other, the
female worshipper, ready to admire at any distance.

12

Madame Helma threw her cloak over one of the deep red velvet chairs, sank majestically into another, and with a move of her ample arm, consigned me to a small brocade and gold affair with very slight spindle legs. The Austrian husband stood by the fireplace and alternately puffed at a cigarette and twisted the ends of his beard and tawny mustache.

Madame preferred to dispense with all preliminary formalities. "Your note said," she began, "that you wished to see me on a matter of a more or less personal nature."

The husband glanced up and took a step toward the door, but madame, with a barely perceptible movement of the wrist, waved him back to the hearth. The husband clicked his heels and bowed to us in turn. "It is more than possible," I said, "that I have made a serious mistake, Madame Helma, and that this visit may prove but an unnecessary annoyance to you."

The eyebrows of madame became somewhat pointed and I saw the husband stealthily pull out his watch.

"I am coming to the point at once," I said. "Did you by any chance ever know a young newspaper man by the name of Hugh Musgrove?" Madame Helma slowly and deliberately bowed her assent. She evidently did not wish to have the young man regarded as one of her intimates.

"I know him but slightly," she said thoughtfully. "You remember him, Louis, surely—the young man that came to interview me after the 'Traviata' matinée, when the draperies caught fire on the stage at the Metropolitan and I saved, oh, so many lives? He also came to tea one day later when we had some other newspaper men."

"I know him well, very well," said the husband. "He was most charming, gracious, and, my dear, how he admired you! What is the matter with the young man?"

"Oh," I said, "you don't know?" Madame Helma was arranging a piece of lace on her corsage, but the husband shook his head.

"He was killed," I said, "in a railroad wreck at Mill's Crossing."

"*Mon Dieu*," said the husband; "what *do* you

14

think of that! He was so young, and how he loved
my Carlotta!"

Madame Helma looked up at her husband questioningly. "I wonder, Louis, if he really did love
me—the poor boy! He was young and not bad looking. I can almost see him now. He sat where you
are sitting—it was but very recently—almost the
other day. And when he talked of my art he really
seemed inspired."

"*Vraiment*," interrupted the husband, "his love
for you, as you say, was inspired. *Le pauvre gar-
çon!*"

"I don't think he loved me at all," Madame
Helma interrupted. "True, he told me how he admired me for having withstood all the temptations
with which every great artist is beset. We are very
temperamental, you know, of course, very temperamental. Many of my sisters in art have succumbed
to their artistic environment, but I have happily remained saturated in the very essence of temperament
and yet withstood its entanglements."

The virtues of Madame Helma seemed fairly
to swell within her and her magnificent physique

to fill the red plush chair even more amply than before.

"I think it was for this," she went on, "and for my position in the social world that Mr. Musgrove really admired me. Don't you remember, Louis, when he told us how he used to go to all my performances and watch the people and their enthusiasm? He spoke particularly of my rendering of 'Dich, theure Halle,' and how the audience rose and cheered me." For a moment Madame Helma became almost human. "I remember he said that that represented to him the very pinnacle of fame; that while the author and the painter might know a more enduring success, the reward came slowly—often after death—while the great opera singer could herself feel the tremendous effect on her audience and receive their homage at almost the same moment. I think it was just fame that that young man craved —fame and glory and the notoriety that goes with it. It was natural, after all, because he really, I suppose, had no fame at all, had he? Louis, you had better send some flowers to his funeral."

"It's too late, I fear," I answered, rising. "The

young man was buried yesterday, and, as you suggest, without ever having attained to any great degree of fame. He was buried from an undertaker's shop on Eighth Avenue."

My mission was at an end. Of the three women whose portraits appeared in the paper, which I still had in my inside pocket, Madame Helma's was the last which I should have imagined would have occupied a young man's thoughts, with death staring him in the face. Nothing, however, would have induced me to show the torn newspaper to Madame Helma, or to have told her how and why it came into my possession. As I reached the door of the apartment, however, it seemed incumbent upon me to say something, which would answer as an apology for my visit.

"I fear, Madame Helma," I said, "that I have intruded upon you needlessly—I knew Hugh Musgrove very slightly, but from an incident in his life I imagined that he was a friend of yours rather than an acquaintance. I was with him when he died, and I thought that you might care to hear more of his end. I must ask your pardon for my error."

Madame Helma was being helped into her mantle by her Austrian husband. We all three bowed somewhat stiffly—I fear I had made them a little late for their dinner. The large presence of Madame Helma had overpowered me, and its spell was still upon me as I wandered down the ill-lit hallway and rang for the elevator. At least, in one thing, she was wise. Musgrove did not love her—in his eyes she stood for fame. And so it seemed his last thoughts were of her, the last face he looked upon was that of Madame Helma—and the face of Madame Helma was to him the sweetest face in all the world, because it was the face of fame and because the lips of fame had never touched his own.

I confess that I was glad to reach the sidewalk and breathe the fresh air again. I turned down Thirty-third Street, and before I had walked a block my feelings, which had been badly ruffled by Madame Helma and her miserable little husband, were pretty well under control. I did not know Hugh Musgrove, but I was really annoyed that any man should have died with the thought of that woman in his brain. As I turned into Broadway, I noticed the clock over

18

the Dime Savings Bank. It was a quarter to seven. "Why not?" I mumbled, and jumped on a north-bound surface car.

I found The Barclay to be like most of the other modern apartment houses that lie north of Forty-second Street and west of Fifth Avenue. On the office floor there was the usual luxurious display of varicolored marble, frescoes, brass railings and large mirrors, but as the elevator shot upward, the colored marble and frescoes gave way to burlap, and at the tenth floor, on which Miss Deane Kimball had her apartment, the walls could boast of but the cheapest kind of wall-paper. As I entered the sitting-room Miss Kimball rose from the table at which she had been eating her dinner. The meal seemed to have been a somewhat frugal one and was served on a napkin-covered tin tray. Miss Kimball nodded to me cheerfully, removed a large cup of coffee from the tray and covered the remnants of her dinner with her napkin.

"You must excuse the condition of the room," she said, "but I have been lying about all day and the girl has had no time to fix it up." She spoke

19

in the low-pitched, drawling voice of the Virginia
bred.

Under the circumstances, it seemed obligatory
upon me to cast one glance about before I could protest that the condition of the room was all it should
be. I found the walls were decorated with many
photographs of Miss Kimball, and, I believe, Miss
Kimball only, although the costumes in which she
had posed were many and varied. There was a tiny
desk, a few lounging chairs, and a cozy-corner strewn
with copies of the evening newspapers. In the general tidiness of her appearance Miss Kimball scarcely
rose superior to that of her surroundings. She wore
a black silk underskirt, a pink dressing-sack covered
with much imitation lace, and her great mass of red
hair was sadly dishevelled. She was one of the few
women I had ever seen whose physical attractions,
judged from a purely material standpoint, admitted
of no discussion. Her color was as clear, her eyes
as bright, her figure as lithe, every move of her arms
and body as supple as that of an athlete. Her dress
may have been careless, but her condition was superb.

"Won't you sit down?" she said. "I'll have to

go to the theatre pretty soon." She walked over to the fireplace and looked at herself in the glass. She ran the white tapering fingers of both hands through the heavy mass of hair. "I'm a sight," she said, but as she said it, I looked into the mirror and saw her smiling at her own beauty.

She returned to the table, and still standing, raised with both hands the heavy china cup of coffee to her lips and sipped at it slowly. Her manner seemed to me to be more casual than familiar. It was as if I had known her always and had dropped in to discuss our party of the night previous. If she had ever understood that I had called on her with a definite purpose in view, such an idea was apparently wholly foreign to her now. But the time was short, and so I came to the point at once.

"Miss Kimball," I said, "did you ever know Hugh Musgrove?" She turned her big smiling eyes on me over the rim of the cup, and took a particularly long sip of coffee.

"I certainly did," she said. "I should say I did know Hugh Musgrove. He was killed in that wreck the other day. I'd have gone to his funeral only I thought there would propably be a lot of newspaper boys there and they might feature me. I wasn't looking for that kind of ad. He'd have got all the advertising he wanted when my divorce comes up next month. Now he's gone, they probably won't mention his name at the trial at all. If I'd gone to the funeral that might all have come out, mightn't it? I sent him a pillow of roses without a card, or a motto, or anything on it. I heard the tributes were all right."

The door opened and a girl walked in. Her dark, glossy hair was heavily marcelled and she wore a black cloth coat and a closely fitting white flannel skirt. She stopped at the doorway while she stuck a hat-pin through the crown of a broad black hat. Miss Kimball introduced her as "My friend from the end of the hall—Miss Wilmot." The girl nodded to me, walked over to the window, and looked out on the brick court. She had heavy, handsome features and an olive complexion and her face seemed incapable of showing any emotion whatever.

"Hurry up, Deane," she said; "it's time to start for the theatre."

"I should say I did know Hugh Musgrove."

"The bubble's not here yet," answered Miss Kimball, sitting down at the table, "and I've only got to change my skirt. I'm not going out after the show. This gentleman knew Hugh."

"I did not know him very well, but I happened to be with him when he died," I said half apologetically, although an apology seemed rather superfluous.

Miss Wilmot continued to look out on the court and beat a slow tattoo on the window-pane. "He was a good boy," she said. "He liked Deane."

Miss Kimball intertwined her fingers behind her head and gazed up at the chandelier. "Yes, he liked me all right," she said reflectively. "You see, he used to come up here and sit of an afternoon when he was tired after the office. It was a sort of home to him. He could smoke a cigarette and play the piano if he wanted to. Why, I'd known Hugh Musgrove all my life. We used to play together in Richmond when we were kids. He lived right around our corner. His folks were splendid people—no better in Richmond. We used to spin tops and jump rope together, and prisoners' base it was we used to play."

"That's why he didn't like getting mixed up in

the divorce," Miss Wilmot interrupted. "Did you know that, Deane? Sure as you're born, that's what he told me."

"What?"

"Why, that no gentleman ought to ever be mixed up in a divorce suit with a girl he'd spun tops with. He said it was worse than cheating at cards."

Miss Kimball stretched her well-rounded arms in front of her on the table. "He did, eh? Now what do you think of that? He *was* a queer kid. He was sort of cheap, and yet, in his way, he was all right. He was a comfortable sort of person to have around."

The telephone bell rang and Miss Wilmot crossed the room and took off the receiver. "It's the electric, Deane," she said. "Hurry up; we're late now!"

Miss Kimball sat unmoved, her pink arms in front of her. Then she turned questioningly to me. "You didn't know him well, you said?"

I nodded.

"Well, now, I'll tell you. He was the kind of man if you needed money and sent out a hurry call or a circular letter, you could always depend on him. Not much—but a five or ten—and the friends that

could give up a yellow-back and not feel it would forget you. You know what I mean?"

Miss Kimball pulled herself together and glanced
up at the scowling face of Miss Wilmot. "You
want to go—don't you, May? Can't we drop you
some place?" she added, turning to me.

"You're very good," I said; "but I'm not going
far."

"No? Hughey was very fond of the bubble—
anything with soft cushions and that came easy. He
was a bit of a loafer, Hughey. Was there anything
else you wanted to know about him?" Miss Kimball
got up from the table and held out her hand. "Glad
to have met you. Don't make yourself strange. I
suppose you come to the theatre sometimes?"

"Yes, I shall come even more often now," I said.
I shook her slim, well-cared-for hand, bowed to Miss
Wilmot, and took my leave.

As I again passed through the marble hallway of
The Barclay I could not, even had I wished it, throw
off completely the spell of the woman upstairs; the
low purr of her voice, the wonderful animal beauty
of her face and hair, and, above all, the indolent

grace of her, were just as evident to me then as they were when I was in the same room with her. I saw her often afterward on the stage, which seemed, after all, to be the niche which nature had carved out for her. It was not easy to conceive, for instance, the dimpled arms pushing a perambulator, or the high, silk-clad instep working the pedal of a sewing-machine. As a picture framed by a proscenium arch and lit by a row of footlights, Miss Deane Kimball was a superb, vital force, and if the last thoughts of the somewhat human Mr. Musgrove harked back to the days of her *regime*, it is for each one to censure or praise, as the case may be.

It was just eight o'clock the next night when I got off a Broadway car at Eighth Street and walked slowly west toward Sixth Avenue, looking up at the dingy doorways for the number of the house of Miss Agnes Beach. I found it at last—a fine example of the old New York home. Its faded brick front with brown-stone trimmings was flanked on one side by a cheap *table-d'hôte* restaurant and on the other by a delicatessen shop. With its polished windows and well-scrubbed steps, the old mansion seemed to hold a place of much dignity in that decayed and unkempt neighborhood. Isolated and forgotten, the very name of its street taken from it, the old place stood there protesting against the changes of the last fifty years and the squalor they had brought to its door. I climbed the steep, worn steps and pulled at the little bell, sunk deep in its round brass socket. An old man with white hair opened the door and stood bowing before me in the broad hallway. He wore a dressing-gown of quilted silk tied about his waist with a cord with tassels at the ends of it. As I stepped into the hallway I looked beyond to a broad stairway and walls and curtains of faded red. It occurred to me, at the time, as the only background possible for the old man with the white hair and the quilted dressing-gown.

"You are the gentleman, I presume," he said, "who wrote my niece in regard to that terrible disaster."

"Your niece is Miss Agnes Beach, then?" I asked.

The old man bowed. "She and her father have their apartments on the floor above. If you will kindly follow me——" The old man started slowly up the stairway, leaning heavily on the balustrade. Apparently, then, I was expected, and perhaps, after all, I had done well to make this third visit. I could easily understand that the members of this household were not accustomed to receive unusual letters from unknown young men, and that the visit of a stranger was, without question, an event of some moment. A single hanging gas-burner lit us on our way up the long stairway. Our shoes sunk noiselessly into the deep faded carpet and the complete silence of the place oppressed me. For a moment I halted on the stairway, listening for the rumble of a cart, the jangle of a car-bell, or the cry of a newsboy from the world outside, but through the heavy walls of the old house no sound reached me. Surely, then, I had found isolation itself and the most cruel loneliness of all—the loneliness of a great city.

The old man knocked gently at the door at the head of the landing, and his brother, in appearance and in the courtesy of his manner, his very counterpart, bowed me graciously into the sitting-room. There was but little light—only a lamp on the centre-table, but as I entered I saw a girl rise from the shadows of a far corner and come to greet me. She was dressed in deep mourning, and even in the dim light I could see her drawn face and the heavy shadows under her eyes. When she reached the centre table she stopped and held out a white hand toward me. In the soft glow of the lamp I saw again the face of the girl with the violin. There was the same childish beauty, the same sincerity and sweetness, but added to all this there was a pathos, an unconscious plea for human pity.

"You were with Hugh when he died?" she asked.

"Yes," I said, "I was with him until the very end."

Through her clouded eyes she looked up at me as if, indeed, mine had been a great privilege.

"He—he didn't suffer much?" she whispered.

"No," I said. "I thought you would want to know that the end came very quickly and very peacefully." The dull-yellow glare from the lamp suddenly seemed to flare up before me and I saw a young man sitting with his back resting against a tree on a hillside. The whole place was bathed in yellow sunlight and the air was full of the smell of springtime, but through it all I saw the face of the young man, ashen and twisted. I felt the girl's hand loosen in my own, and so I grasped it tightly, and the contact of it brought me back to the lamp at my side and the girl in black and the old man standing silently at the door.

"You knew him before, then?" she asked.

"No," I said, "I never knew him before."

The girl looked up at me as if she could not quite understand how it was that every one had not known Hugh Musgrove. "He was very good to know," she said. And then the very inadequacy of her words forced a smile to her pale lips. "And he was very fine," she added, "and true—and he was so very—so very good to dad and me."

"I wish I could have told you more," I said.

The girl nodded her head. "You told me what I wished most to know. I am so glad you came."

Her hand, nerveless and cold, dropped from my own and I bowed myself to the door. Her father closed it softly behind us and led me down the broad stairway to his brother's apartment on the ground floor. With much courtesy my host asked me to be seated at a centre-table, about which three chairs

"You told me what I wished most to know."

had been placed. On the polished surface of the old mahogany there were three glasses, a decanter of port and some crackers in a silver cake-basket. The host poured out the wine and after raising our glasses we drank in silence. The father of Miss Beach leaned across the table and laid his hand gently on my arm.

"You must not be hurt, sir, if my daughter gave you but a scant welcome," he said. "Youth is always intolerant, you know, and she is very young. Her mother died when the girl was only a child, and this is her first tragedy. She cannot quite understand why it should have come to her." The old man hesitated for a moment and apparently unconsciously raised the glass to his lips.

"Perhaps you did not know," he went on, "that Hugh was engaged to my daughter—it was just about to be announced. If all went well they were to be married in the fall. He was her life—he and her music. They played together almost every night. I used to accompany her, but then Hugh came and she would allow only him to play for her, although I have been a music-teacher for many years, and he —well, he did not play very well. She was quite

31

deaf to his mistakes—love, you know, they say, is blind, and I have thought it was often deaf, too. He really played, oh, so badly. But it was wonderful to see the lights in her eyes when she took the bow in her hand and waited for Hugh to play the first notes. And now she is so tired and frail and the color is gone—she is as white as we two old men." He stopped for a moment and with his elbow on the table rested his chin in the palm of his hand.

"But Hugh was of great help to her," he went on. "He knew many of the most famous musical people in town, and it was really through him that Agnes was to make her *début* with the Philharmonic."

"And now?" I asked.

The old man looked up in much surprise at my question. "Now?" he repeated. "She says she will never play again. She says that her love for her violin died with him. But she is young, you know, and I think that in time she may find a certain consolation in her music. It was the same with me. I, too, put away my music, but the time came when our wants forced me to take it up again."

The old man raised his glass and looked down

into the dark red-colored wine. "But I don't think the music was ever quite the same."

It seemed to me that Mr. Beach had said all that he had wished to say to me, and so I rose to go. It was at this moment that I remembered that the torn page from the supplement was still in my pocket.

"Do you think it would be possible," I asked, "to see your daughter again for a moment?"

"You will find that she is still in the sitting-room, I am sure," he said.

As I went up the stairway again, but this time alone, I took out the half-page of the newspaper and carefully tearing off the part containing the picture of Miss Beach, put the rest back in my pocket. I found her standing at the piano, and as I entered she looked up at me, dry-eyed, and with almost a smile of welcome on her lips.

"I know you'll pardon me," I said, "but I had very nearly forgotten the real object of my visit. I wanted to give you this piece of paper. Just before his death I saw him take it from his pocket and look at it. It was the last face he ever saw—his last thoughts were of her."

The girl took the torn piece of paper from my hand, but she did not look at it. There was surely no doubt in her mind who was the original of the portrait.

I found the two old men waiting for me in the hall-way downstairs. We saluted each other gravely and parted with proper ceremony. The door closed noiselessly behind me as I walked slowly down the steps and stopped irresolutely on the curbstone. Directly across the street there was a cheap French restaurant. Through the open window I saw two young men playing dominoes at a marble table, and a waiter with a dirty apron leaning over the counter smiling at the woman cashier. Everything, after those two old men and the girl in black whom I had just left, seemed so soiled and unworthy. I took out of my pocket all there remained of the half-page of the supplement, tore it into small pieces, and threw it into the dirty street. So far as I was concerned, there was an end to it and I knew no more than I had two days before. Perhaps the young girl in the old house back of me was right, and there could only have been one thought in Musgrove's mind, and that was of her. But it may have been that he looked last at the portrait of Madame Helma, whose world-wide fame he envied so, or perhaps it was that of Miss Kimball, of the Cockatoo chorus, whose physical beauty he had evidently, too, admired very greatly. And as I started to retrace my steps along the dingy streets on my way back to the lights of Broadway, I wondered, too, whether he had thrown that paper away because he was ashamed to die with it, or was it out of thoughtfulness for the fair name of some woman.

"BEAUTY" KERRIGAN

"BEAUTY" KERRIGAN

As the old man reached the doorway of the burning building, the woman threw herself upon him and, seizing him by the shoulders, wheeled him back toward her.

"I tell you they're not in the flat," she shrieked above the roar of the flames. "Katie told me she was goin' across the hall to the Cassidys."

The old man stood staring at his wife with his mouth wide open and his arms hanging impotently in front of him. "I thought they was to home," he mumbled—"honest, I thought they was to home."

Kerrigan picked his way over the network of hose to the old couple, and shaking the man, tried to rouse him from his stupor. "What's up?" he asked briskly.

The old man, with wide frightened eyes, looked up at the young one, but his tongue refused to move, so he raised both arms and waved them toward the burning tenement. But it was different with the woman. There was an assurance in Kerrigan's manner, and a certain eagerness in his eyes, that made her believe him to be some one in authority, and so she seized him by the broad shoulders and pulled him down to her, so that she could shout in his ear. "My kids are in there—they'll be burned alive. The old man told the fireman they was in the third floor front, but I know they was at Cassidy's across the hall in the rear building."

Kerrigan stepped back and looked up at the high tenement with its gridiron of iron fire-escapes. The upper stories were shut out now by clouds of heavy black smoke, but the windows of the second and third stories flared up like the open doors of a blast furnace. Above the confused din of shouting firemen, the hissing shriek of escaping steam, the clanging of bells from the third-alarm engines, and the warning cries of the crowd, there arose the continuous roar and the sharp crackle of unconquered flames. A hose burst almost at Kerrigan's feet and the sting of the cold water in his face once more stirred him into action.

He seized the old woman and put his mouth to her ear. "The third floor back?" he shouted. The woman nodded her head at him, and then in her frenzy turned to the crowds pressing against the ropes. "For God's sake," she shrieked, "won't somebody tell those firemen about my kids!" A passing fireman stopped at the woman's cry. "Have you got kids in there?" he asked. The old woman only shook her head and with her arms beat the air in the direction of the flames.

"Well, you got to get out of this," the man said; "that wall is liable to go any time now. The roof's gone and the floors are givin' away already." With both hands he half led, half dragged the old couple away from the building, and with the aid of a policeman finally forced them behind the ropes.

In the meantime Kerrigan stood looking into the open doorway of the burning tenement. The fire had not yet reached the lower floor, and it was quite possible that he could find the fireman who had gone for the children and tell them that they were in the back of the house. The front of the building was a raging furnace, but there was a slight chance that it might be better in the rear. For a moment he hesitated, then he pulled his hat down hard and ran for the open doorway. Inside there was a pale gray smoke that smarted his eyes, and so he shut them tight and promptly fell over a hose. He knew that this must lead him to the firemen, and so with one hand on the throbbing rubber and the other one feeling against the wall, he groped his way along the narrow hall-way. Half-way down the passage he found the stair-way. The smoke was much thicker here and the roar of the flames and the crackling of the timber overhead was quite deafening, but the hose led him on up the winding staircase. For a moment Kerri-gan opened his eyes and through a rift in the smoke he was almost sure that he saw the outline of a figure at the next landing. He clutched the banisters with both hands and called aloud, but his voice seemed to have lost all of its power, his eyes smarted terribly, and the awful heat was becoming unbearable.

Outside in the sunlit streets a half-grown girl pushed and fought her way through the dense crowd of onlookers massed behind the fire lines. "Mother!" she shrieked to the old woman, who was still calling on some one to rescue her children. "Mother, shut up, won't you—the kids are over to Myer's drug store."

"Glory be to God," whispered the old woman and doubled up over the rope in front of her. And as she did so the upper half of the front wall of the burning building wavered, while the crowd shouted its warning and the grimy, rubber-coated firemen raced toward the crowd for safety. For a moment the great wall of brick and iron ladders staggered in mid-air and then with a sullen roar fell backward and crashed its way through the burning floors.

The lights had already begun to twinkle in the skyscrapers when the four men gathered about the city desk that night and talked of the Canal Street fire and the past, the present and the future of "Beauty" Kerrigan. Through the open windows there came from the park below the shrill cries of the newsboys, the rumble of the elevated trains and the rush of many hurrying footsteps. The tall building trembled slightly and then settled to the ceaseless throbbing of the presses down in the basement throwing out the night edition. The City Editor shut his watch with a noisy click. "It won't do," he said —"it won't do. We've got to get this paper out earlier or get out ourselves. Did any of you see Kerrigan?"

"I saw what was left of 'Beauty' under a blanket on the way to the ambulance," The Cub volunteered. "He was all covered up. Fielding was with him, though; took him to the hospital, I guess, while I was chasing the old woman that thought her kids were in the building. That wide-eyed boy that reports fires and conventions for the *Tribune* told me that was what took 'Beauty' into the house—to tell the firemen where the kids were."

"That's just like Kerrigan," the Copy Reader interrupted. "With every respect to a man in the hospital 'Beauty' certainly had a high regard for the limelight. He ought to have been an actor."

The City Editor put his feet on the desk and clasping his hands behind his head, looked up at the cobwebbed ceiling. "I liked Kerrigan," he said. "I know what you mean, but he'd been called a Greek God so long and so often that he began to believe he was a little differently made from the rest of us. Whatever happens to him it happened while he was trying to save a couple of kids he never saw. You can't take that away from him."

"I tell you, boys," interrupted the Sporting Editor, "you're all in wrong. He wasn't stuck on himself, but he loved health and condition just as any of you love a piece of mince pie. He'd played on that Western college ball team of his for four years, and the football team, too, and he'd kept himself hard ever since. He didn't smoke and he didn't drink, but that didn't make him any the less of a man. He was no more stuck on his Greek head than you are on yours, but he did believe a man's body is a nice bit of machinery to take care of, not a receptacle for every violet-colored liqueur that comes from Paris, France. I tell you I know the boy."

"All right," said the Copy Reader, "but not for mine. His friend Fielding, that thinks so much of him, is worth two of 'Beauty,' and can write better stuff with his left hand. I know, because I read all they write."

The City Editor continued to look up at the ceiling. "Kerrigan was a little up in the air sometimes," he said; "he was a bad reporter and Fielding is a good man—that is, to get facts. Kerrigan had too much imagination—he's a fiction writer. I'll bet you now that Bert Fielding will be a reporter when Kerrigan is among the best six sellers—that is, if he lives."

"Look out!" said The Cub—"here's Fielding now."

A young man came into the office, walked over to a desk and picked up some letters and then joined the four men.

"How's 'Beauty'?" asked the City Editor.

Fielding sat on a desk and shook his head. "Oh, I don't know—nobody knows anything—yet. They wouldn't let me see him, but I hear he's all smashed up and burned, too, terribly. We've got to wait—that's all." Fielding clasped his hands together and pressed them between his knees. Then he looked slowly about him at each of the four men in turn. "I tell you, it's hell to see those young doctors at the hospital standing around there smiling and so cool in their damned white suits and not able to do anything. They're all right, I guess, but the worst of it is I can't do anything."

"I suppose—I suppose they'll make him comfortable," The Cub suggested. Fielding nodded. "That's all right—Kerry has a little money of his own."

"Isn't there some one we ought to send for?" asked the City Editor.

Fielding brushed his sleeve sharply across his eyes. "Not that I know of," he said. "I've lived with him for five years and he never mentioned any relatives to me. He's alone just like I am."

The City Editor got up and laid his hand on Fielding's shoulder. "Try to take it easy, old man," he said. "It may all come out right. Better go now and have a little dinner with us."

Fielding put out his hand and turned away his head. "Thank you, but not now. I said I'd call up the hospital a little later. They seemed to think they might know something then."

The four men gathered about him and each in his own way tried to show his sympathy, and then they said good-night and left him sitting alone in the deserted room. For some moments he sat swinging his legs on the desk and looking wide-eyed out into space. Then he pulled himself together and went over to the open window. There was the scent of the early spring in the air and a few silver stars were twinkling through the purple sky. Fielding looked up at the stars and shook his head. "But why 'Beauty' Kerrigan," he asked, "of all the men in the world—why 'Beauty'? Life and health and good looks meant so much more to him than the rest of us. Just suppose You should let him live—just suppose that?"

It was late one evening the following June when Fielding led a muffled figure through the long corridors of the hospital to the cab waiting on the hot, deserted street. Broken and twisted and scarred, Kerrigan, even with the help of a cane and his friend's arm, shuffled along but slowly and with much effort. Before they started on that long, portentous journey of two hours, Fielding had received his final instructions in the private office of the head doctor.

"Internally," said the little great man, carefully weighing each word, "he is as well as you or I—he may outlive either or both of us. You understand it is just as if you had smashed the case of a beautiful watch, but the works had been left unimpaired. I think he had the best frame and the best constitution I ever met with in a long practice—of course, it was these that pulled him through. What he will need now, and you must try very hard to help him to it, is courage—always courage. Courage to look into a mirror—courage to forget. And, above all, try to keep up his interest in things and make him work, work continuously—the more the better."

"I understand, doctor," said Fielding, "and I'll try very hard." Then he found his friend and together they started on their journey.

The stars were out and a young silver moon hung over them when they reached the little town of Pleasant Harbor. John Ferguson, the old Scotchman, who was to be Kerrigan's servant, met them at the station and drove them in a closed carriage to the home that Fielding had prepared. During the past summer Kerrigan and Fielding had driven from the hotel in the village over this road many times, and on just such nights as this, sometimes alone, when they always planned to buy the white farmhouse for their old age; and more often they had driven with young girls, who laughed and sang with them, just from the animal happiness of health and the sheer joy of living.

They found Mary Ferguson, the wife of John Ferguson, the Scotchman, standing in the doorway, her broad, buxom frame silhouetted against the square of yellow light that flooded the room beyond. It would have been her wish to have followed the men into the long low sitting-room, because she would have liked to have seen their pleasure over all the beautiful flowers and ferns she had gathered in honor of Kerrigan's home-coming. However, she did not follow the two friends, who, arm in arm, entered the house alone. For a few moments Kerrigan stood resting on his cane and looking about at the gray wall-paper, with its delicate tracing of yellow flowers, at the bright chintz curtains and the old mahogany furniture, all newly covered in green leather, and the wood shining like burnished brass in the orange light of the shaded lamps. In one corner of the room, just by the window that looked out on the meadow and the river beyond, they had placed a broad desk, with all Kerrigan's writing things on it, and besides these a great bowl of crimson ramblers. The desk was flanked on either side by his books, and in the pictures on the walls he found none but old friends.

He reached out his hand and laid it on Fielding's arm. "It's all quite wonderful, Bert," he said—"quite wonderful, just like sunshine—and that's good, because you see this room is my whole world now."

And this as events turned out was largely true. As the long days passed Kerrigan seldom left the house, and then only very late in the evening, when Ferguson drove him in a closed carriage over the deep, sandy roads. Sometimes, on a Saturday night, when Fielding had come down to stop over Sunday, the two friends would go out sailing in their little cat-boat, but these were Kerrigan's only excursions abroad. The people of Pleasant Harbor had never seen the mysterious stranger who lived in the old farmhouse up the river, and, indeed, so long as he paid his bills they were willing to forget the presence of their neighbor, just as he wished to be forgotten. The children of the village, however, were not so indifferent to the newcomer and chose to believe that the only occupant of the house, besides the Scotchman and his wife, was a perfectly well-defined ghost. They spoke of the old farmhouse now in whispers, and called it "haunted," and always ran by the place at night, although the house stood far back from the road. To prove their point, they told of how a mysterious crooked figure with a black cloak had been sailing on the river, and at other times huddled in the back of a carriage, and how, very late one moonlight night, the same cloaked, crooked figure had been discovered wandering over the golf links of the "summer folks" and occasionally stopping and making curious slow motions with his cane in the air, just as a real ghost would do were he playing golf with an invisible ball.

The Scotchman went to the post-office for the mail every morning and again at night, and sometimes he received long bulky letters, and at other times small thin ones, with the name of some publishing house in the corner; but all of these letters were addressed to John Ferguson. The accounts at the village were paid by checks signed by the same name, and later on the name of John Ferguson began to appear as an occasional contributor in the better

class of magazines. As a living being, "Beauty"
Kerrigan had stepped aside the day of the Canal
Street tenement fire and had let the world pass on.
As a human being, he existed only for Fielding and
his two servants; as a writer, he was slowly gaining a
place of honorable distinction, but the tributes to
fame that he had envied so in others, the tinsel success that he had hoped and worked and prayed for in
his youthful days, now that it was almost within his
grasp, could never be his, because "Beauty" Kerrigan did not exist in the eyes of the world. "My home
is my tomb," he said once, and he believed it. To
his friend he spoke but little of his work, and indeed
Fielding usually read it for the first time when it
appeared in the magazines under the name of John
Ferguson.

But late in the spring of Kerrigan's first year at
Pleasant Harbor, he told Fielding of a drama he
wanted to write. To be the author of a successful
play had always been his ambition, and now be believed that it was time to move on toward that accomplishment. He had the scenario well mapped out,
even the minor characters had taken shape and

character in his mind, and he had already written some of the dialogue for the "great" scene in the second act.

And so, for the next few months, Kerrigan gave up the short stories and the special articles and devoted himself to his drama. Every Sunday he would read over to Fielding his week's work, and his friend, who had a slight practical knowledge of the stage, would make suggestions and revisions.

In the early fall Fielding carried the manuscript back with him to New York and gave it to the dramatic editor of his paper, who, he knew, could at least obtain for it the serious consideration of the managers. It was a month later when he wired to Kerrigan one morning that a manager had made an appointment with him to talk over the play. "It may amount to nothing," he said at the end of his message, "but there is a chance."

The manager sat behind a very large flat desk and divided his time about equally between talking slowly and silently rolling a long cigar between his lips. The well-thumbed manuscript of the play lay on the desk in front of him, and during the conversation he occasionally ran a paper-cutter between its pages and tapped it thoughtfully on the blue cover.

"I don't want to produce this play, very much," he said, by way of introduction, "and I don't say that to get better terms. Personally, I don't think there is any money in it, and Miss Carew, who wants to play it, will get very little out of it but reputation, and I will probably lose something. I don't know who the author is, but I should say that it was a man, and one who knew very little of the stage—that is, its practical side. He has written two women parts, of almost equal strength, and that is, as you probably know, almost fatal. But Miss Carew wants to play the part of 'Ellen,' and I know why she wants to play it. It is what we call an actor's part—it is the sort of part any actress would enjoy playing before critics or at a professional matinée. And about the same thing might be said about the 'Millicent' part. If I had a play which would give Miss Carew nearly as good a chance as 'Ellen,' and still have the popular element in it, I should not think of trying your piece, but I haven't. I candidly don't think this is going to be popular, but it is not an expensive play to put on, and I have decided to take a chance. I will give you five hundred dollars in advance and five per cent. on the gross. That is not as much as the big ones get, but I imagine the author is a beginner and he could hardly expect more."

Fielding nodded. "I can answer for the author that the terms will be all right. When do you think we can get a production?"

"At once," said the manager, briskly—"the sooner the better. This piece Miss Carew is playing now won't do at all. I should like to begin rehearsals immediately. The necessary changes can be made as we go along. Can the author come to rehearsals?"

Fielding shook his head: "I'm afraid not," he said.

"Is he alive?"

"Yes."

"Far away?"

"No, not far," Fielding said. "It's hard to explain."

"It's hard on us, too. As I said before, the play must be changed in a number of places to be effective. I don't want to give the good lines to Miss Carew and weaken the other parts, because we have both

agreed that this can't be done; but I must have the
author's help. He may think his work is over, but if
he knew more about this business, he would know
that it has just begun. I'm sorry to insist, but I
wouldn't care to go on without him. It would mean
calling in some play-carpenter, who would probably
spoil the atmosphere and ruin such chances as the
piece has now."

"Very good," said Fielding, "will you give me
until to-morrow noon?"

"Sure—if you can let me know the author's answer then. Come in, and we can sign the contracts
and start on the scenery and rehearsals at once.
Good-day!"

Fielding did not wait for the elevator, but went
down the marble stairway two steps at a bound.
Then he took a cab for the ferry and a half hour later
was on the express for Pleasant Harbor. He found
Kerrigan waiting for him in the sitting-room. "It's
all right!" he cried, "it's all right! You're going to
get the production. Miss Carew is going to do it as
soon as they can get ready. Just think of it, your first
play and to be done on Broadway—it's wonderful!"

Kerrigan stood looking at him from across the room as if he could not quite comprehend the full extent of the fortune that had come to him. Then he limped over to the door with the little window and looked out on the river. Since the first days when he had begun to write for his college paper, he had looked forward to this moment. To write a play and have it produced in New York by a successful star had always seemed to him the greatest happiness that could come to any man. The amount of money he might thus earn had hardly occurred to him—it was the fame he courted. It was the cry of "author" he craved—the lights and the excitement and the thrill of facing that great critical audience across the footlights. And now it had all come true, this dream of the days of his youth and health. It would all happen just as he had planned and hoped, but he would not sit in the stage box and he would not make the speech before the curtain after the "big" scene in the second act. Instead he would look out on the river that night from this little room of his, and he would be quite alone.

Fielding knew as well all that was passing in Ker-

rigan's mind as if his friend had been speaking aloud
to him. And so he waited until the cripple shuffled
over to his deep leather chair by the hearth.

"And I got pretty good terms, too, I think,
Kerry," he said—"five hundred in advance!"

Kerrigan nodded, and for some moments the two
men sat looking at the burning logs on the broad
hearth.

"But there is one thing," Fielding said at last,
"that worries me a good deal. Bronson says there
must be some trifling changes made at rehearsal. It
seems there are certain places where the play is not
quite right—that is, not practical."

Kerrigan nodded. "Of course, of course, I expected that, but I can make the changes down here."

For a moment Fielding hesitated. "I'm sorry,
Kerry," he said, "but Bronson insists that the author
must come up to town and work with him. He practically makes it a condition if he accepts the play."

Kerrigan looked at Fielding, but apparently with
unseeing eyes. "It's too bad!" he said. "I should
like very much to have had the production." For a
long time the only sound in the room came from the

crackle of the logs, and then Kerrigan put out his hand and laid it gently on Fielding's arm and looked him in the eyes. "Won't you go for me? You understand—be the author."

Fielding looked at his friend and smiled, and then stretched his arms above his head. "Why, Kerry," he said, "you know I couldn't do that, not even for you! Anything you can ask of me but that!"

"I understand," Kerrigan said, "but who else is there? You are the only person who knows what the play means and how it ought to be played. You could come down here at night and we could make the changes together, and write in any new scenes or speeches they needed. You can be 'John Ferguson' as well as I—and it's only to a few people. You know you had a lot to do with the play, as it is. You were such a help—won't you go on with it, please?" Kerrigan slipped slowly back into his deep chair and looked at the flames and waited.

Fielding sat with his arms tightly folded across his breast and staring up at a portrait over the hearth. Then his eyes turned to the bent figure lying in the chair at his side. "All right, Kerry," he said, "that's all right; I'll be the author—'John Ferguson'—for a few weeks."

The rehearsals of the new play—"The Interpreter," by John Ferguson—had been going on for about a week, when Miss Carew called, by appointment, at the office of her manager.

"What do you think?" Bronson asked abruptly.

Miss Carew pursed her pretty lips and frowned thoughtfully at the tip of her patent-leather boot. "I think it's all right," she said. "I don't believe there is a possibility of its not making a success—that is in an artistic way; it's a beautiful play. The critics will like it—nobody knows what the public is going to do. It may be a little sad for them, but it seems to me there is a tremendous human appeal in it, especially in the part of 'Millicent.'"

"I know that—that's why I sent for you. You remember I told you."

Miss Carew nodded at Bronson and smiled. "I know you did," she said. "Where did you get her? I heard her say she'd never been on Broadway."

Bronson could not restrain a broad smile of self-appreciation. "I heard about her work and her good looks when she was here at a dramatic school. I didn't take much stock in it, but I went to see her at one of their performances and signed her up the same afternoon. Then I sent her out West to do one-night stands. I got her to go in stock at Kansas City all last summer and let her stay there till this came along. But I can take her out yet if you say so. She's young enough to wait, and you know I'm always ready to protect your interests. Speak up if you want me to get some one else—not quite so strong."

Miss Carew shook her head. "That's all right," she said, and held out a white-gloved hand. "I don't mind if the play makes a hit—besides I need the money."

Bronson bustled out of his swivel chair and patted his star affectionately on the back. "You're a good girl, Blanche," he said, and taking her arm started her toward the door, "you're a good girl." Miss Carew stopped in the doorway and smiled over her shoulder at the manager, who had returned to his desk and was puffing great clouds of smoke from a freshly lit cigar. "You got through that a good deal better than you expected," she called, "didn't you?"

"A good deal better," he said, laughing, "a good deal better!"

Fielding had obtained a leave of absence from his paper for three weeks, and during the morning and afternoon hours he sat down in front at Bronson's favorite theatre and watched the rehearsals of the play of which he was supposed to be the author. He saw it grow and develop and become a perfect whole; he saw actors and actresses who began by stumbling through their lines, gradually grow into the men and women that Kerrigan in his little room at Pleasant Harbor had bred, and to whom he had given minds and souls and human passions. For the most part Fielding sat in the deserted orchestra, but sometimes he went back on the stage and told some particular player just what a line or a situation meant, and often they sought him out and asked for his advice. But the girl who probably needed his help the least, and yet to whom he went and who came to him the most often, was the girl who played "Millicent," and who, as the character-man said when the rehearsals first began, was going to "score, and score good."

Even to the unpracticed eye of Fielding there was not much in common between this young girl, this Ruth Emery, and her fellow players. The ways of the stage-folk were not yet her ways. She seemed to have acquired all the ambition and hope that had long since been crushed out of their lives by years of hard toil, and for which they had earned so little of honor or accomplishment.

"She's wonderful!" he said to Kerrigan one night after a long day of rehearsing—"she's quite wonderful! They all run about and shout at her and she just goes on being 'Millicent.' I could stand it all if you could only see *her* that first night. We go out to a little place around the corner every day now for lunch together and she never talks of anything but the play." Kerrigan smiled. "And the playwright?" he asked.

"Oh, you don't understand, Kerry, really you don't. She doesn't care about men, especially me. It's just the play. You know it's a great chance for a young girl. She's really helped me with suggestions more than I have her."

"Is she—is she pretty?"

"Pretty? She's a wonder—not like anybody you ever saw. She promised to bring me some photographs to-morrow. I knew you would want to see how she looked, so I'll bring them down to-morrow night."

"And Miss Carew?"

"Fine—really splendid, but she's different, that's all!"

"Good-night!" Kerrigan said. "Good-night, old man. I was sure something would make you forgive me for making you a playwright. I didn't know it would be Miss Emery, but it's all right so long as you're happy. Don't forget the photographs."

And Fielding, true to his promise, did not forget the photographs, but brought them down the next night, and, to the exclusion of many old friends, they were given the places of honor in the little white cottage. On the very large photograph there was written: "To the Author of 'The Interpreter' with the sincere appreciation of Ruth Emery," and this was placed on the mantel over the fireplace; the smaller picture bore the one word—"Ruth"—and this was, by mu-

tual consent, carried to Fielding's own room under
the rafters.

For Fielding those three weeks of rehearsal were
three weeks of the most intense excitement and of a
complete happiness he had ever known. He watched
with increasing anxiety the play reach the point
where it was only necessary to add the finishing
touches and to work on the most exacting scenes.
He looked on at the making of the properties, the
arrangement of the lights and the building of the
scenery, and every morning and evening he searched
eagerly for the preliminary notices as they gradually
crept into the newspapers. Every afternoon he took
a late train to Pleasant Harbor, and once there it was
necessary to tell Kerrigan all that had taken place at
rehearsal, what every one had said and done, and
what he thought every one had thought of his or her
lines and the play. And then after dinner they worked
on the changes which Bronson thought necessary.
Kerrigan sat at his desk and made notes, and Fielding stalked about the floor, and by reading the old
lines and the new tried to show how it would appear
on the stage. Sometimes they worked for an hour or

two and sometimes until far into the morning. Several times they had written and talked until the sun rose, and it really seemed hardly worth while for Fielding to go to bed at all, so little time remained before his breakfast and the early train to town. And through all this there was always the thought of the girl who had come into his life, with her clear, clean mind and her flower-like beauty, and who had dragged him out of the mental rut of indifference and indolence into which he had gradually fallen. And with the picture of the girl in his mind and the gratitude in his heart for all he owed her, there was always that other thought—the thought that he was not the real "John Ferguson," that he was deceiving her. It may have been a deception inspired by generosity—Kerrigan had called it a sacrifice—but whatever Fielding had won from the girl he had won under false colors, and he knew it and suffered for it.

The dress rehearsal was to take place on the Sunday night preceding the first performance, and Fielding had gone down to pass the early part of the day at Pleasant Harbor. They had spent the morning together going over the newspapers and cutting out the notices from the amusement columns. "We had better save these," Kerrigan said, laughing. "We may never get any more for our scrap-book!"

"I don't know—I don't know," Fielding said, stopping in his tramp up and down the room. "I'm terribly confused. Sometimes I think it is going to be a great success, and then something goes wrong at rehearsal and it all seems hopeless. If it weren't for Miss Emery—not only for her performance—but she does so much to encourage me and keep me going, and helps me so in secretly showing me how to help the others. It is just intelligence against a bag of tricks. She comes with a new brain, fresh and clear, while the heads of the rest of them are filled with a thousand parts they have played or wanted to play, and overburdened with every old tradition of the stage from Shakespeare down to Belasco. As Bronson said to me the other day after Ruth's scene in the first act, 'It will be such a pity when that girl learns how to act.' I tell you, Kerry, you don't know what she has done for that play of yours!"

Kerrigan was looking up at the girl's photograph over the mirror. "Yes," he said slowly, "I think I do, and when it's all over I want you to thank her for me, whether the play is a success or a failure—thank her as I would have thanked her."

The audience that filled the theatre on the first night of "The Interpreter" was, in all ways, worthy of Miss Carew's position as an actress and the reputation of the players with whom Bronson had surrounded her. At the end of the first act the men in the lobbies and those who remained to visit their friends in the orchestra stalls and the boxes agreed that Mr. John Ferguson, whoever he might be, had apparently written a fine play, that Miss Carew was at her best and that Miss Ruth Emery was a distinct "find" for Bronson, the manager. When the curtain came down on the "big" scene in the second act, the play had, beyond question, scored a success and Miss Emery little less than a triumph. There were many curtain calls and the proper acknowledgment from the company, and mingled with the applause there were distinct and evidently sincere calls for the author. But to these calls there was no acknowledgment, for the author was at the time huddled in the back of a closed carriage driving along a heavy, sandy road down by the Natasqua River, and the man who had for the past few weeks acted the part of the author was sitting, very cold and very nervous, in the last row of the balcony.

The telegraph station at Pleasant Harbor closed at eight o'clock in the evening, and so when it was all over, there was nothing for Fielding to do but wait for the morning to tell Kerrigan that "The Interpreter" had achieved a real success. Miss Carew and Bronson had never doubted that the critics would approve of it, and in this their judgment was correct. Some of them even went so far as to say that if Mr. Ferguson had not written the great American play, there was no reason to believe that he might not eventually do so. They also were profuse in their gratitude to Bronson for daring to introduce this new American author, and loud in their praise of Miss Carew for appearing in a play in which she, at best, could but share the honors with another and unknown actress. But the success of the play was not alone confined to the men who wrote the reviews and to whom technique and the literary quality count for

so much. The human note that had appealed to Miss
Carew so strongly found its way over the footlights
to the great theatre-going public, and the public
showed its appreciation by going to see "The Interpreter" for many months, not only in New York, but
all over the country.

When the play was over that first night, and the
theatre was empty, Fielding went down on the stage
and visited the different members of the company in
their dressing-rooms, and thanked them for all the
hard work they had done and the help they had been
to the play. He had arranged, long before that night,
that Miss Emery and he were to take supper together
and talk it all over, but the excitement of her success
had told on the girl, and instead of going to supper,
she asked that he would take her for a drive so that
she could be in the open air. They took a hansom
and drove up Fifth Avenue out to the park, which at
that hour and at that season of the year was quite
deserted. It was a fine clear night, fairly warm for so
late in October, and as they jogged along over the
smooth roads, the girl leaned out over the doors and
drank in long breaths of the clear night air. Fielding

sat back in the hansom and looked at the girl's profile, at the full rounded throat and at the soft brown hair brushed back over the delicately moulded ear. She was the one woman who had ever meant very much to him and she meant everything—the woman who had filled his mind and his heart every hour of every day since he had first known her. He put out his hand and laid it on hers.

"I never knew what happiness really meant before," he said.

"That must mean a good deal—especially to you —to be really happy."

"Why especially to me?" he asked.

The girl was looking out ahead of her, at the winding road and at the rows of dark leafless trees that lined their path. "Oh, I don't know exactly, except the man who wrote 'The Interpreter' could not always have been very happy."

There was a silence for a moment and then Fielding spoke quite evenly and almost without inflection——

"I didn't write 'The Interpreter,'" he said. "No, I did not write 'The Interpreter.'"

The girl turned and looked at him and his eyes met her glance fairly. Then she turned back to her former position, her arms resting on the doors of the hansom.

"Do you care for me," he asked, "or do you care for the author of the play?" It was the first time he had ever spoken of either of them caring for any one.

The girl put up one hand and pressed it gently across her eyes. "I don't quite know—who did write 'The Interpreter?'"

"A friend of mine named Kerrigan. He's a cripple. When he was younger—only a year or so ago—he was very strong and very good-looking. They called him 'Beauty' Kerrigan in those days. He was hurt trying to get some children out of a burning building and afterward he chose to live like a hermit. He doesn't exist except for me."

"Couldn't I see him?" she asked. "I owe him a great deal. I'd like to say 'thank you' to him."

"I don't know—I don't know that," he said. "You see I promised I never would tell, and I've broken my promise. I never would have told any one except you—to-night."

They drove back in silence, and Fielding left her at her boarding-house, and then went on to his own room and waited until it was time to go to Pleasant Harbor. The first train started while the stars were still shining and the sun was not long up when he reached his destination. Kerrigan had not expected him until the first morning express train, which arrived some time after the slow local Fielding had decided to take at the last moment. There was no one at the station to meet him and so he started to walk to the farm, shortening his journey by tramping through the fields, still wet with dew and heavy with the scent of wild flowers.

When he reached the white farmhouse he softly opened the door, believing that Kerrigan was still asleep. But he found him standing in the sitting-room, looking tired and worn as if he, too, had had a bad night. He was leaning against the side of the fireplace and looking at the picture of Ruth Emery, which he held between his two scarred hands. When he heard Fielding he looked up and then slowly put the photograph back in its place.

"Well?" he asked.

74

"BEAUTY" KERRIGAN

Fielding threw a bundle of the morning papers on the desk. "It's fine, Kerry!" he said. "It's a big hit and the papers say your work is wonderful! Bronson and Miss Carew and every one were delighted—absolutely satisfied."

And then the two men sat down before the fire, and Fielding read each notice aloud several times and told Kerrigan everything that had happened, from the rise of the first to the fall of the last curtain and afterward. He told him, too, of his drive with Miss Emery and of all that he had said to her.

"You must see her, Kerry," he begged—"if it's only for a moment. She feels that she owes you so much."

And so, although Kerrigan had not seen nor spoken to a girl since the day of the fire, it was arranged before Fielding went back to town the next day that he was to return on Sunday and bring Miss Emery with him.

It was on a brilliant November morning that they arrived at the little station and found Ferguson waiting for them. A fresh breeze blew in over the water and there was a sharp tang in the air that gave warning of the coming winter and started the blood tingling in their veins. When they reached the white farmhouse Fielding opened the door into Kerrigan's sitting-room and Ruth Emery went in to meet her host. Every curtain had been pulled aside, every shade had been raised so that the place was flooded with sunlight. In the golden haze they found Kerrigan standing in the centre of the room leaning on his cane and waiting. The girl moved quickly across the room with her hand outstretched toward him. Kerrigan tried to stand very erect, but at the touch of her hand he crumpled up and she put her arms about him as if he had been a child. Fielding closed the door softly behind him and walked around the house and over the meadow to the river. When he had reached the pier he got into the cat-boat and quite mechanically hoisted the sail, and casting off went sailing away down the little river.

Those of us who follow the drama most closely believe that the marriage of Ruth Emery deprived the stage of a very exceptional emotional actress, but if she shares this belief, she has certainly never been known to have expressed it. Fielding fell back into his old easy-going and always lovable ways, and is still a valued member of the paper that first employed him. Kerrigan writes plays now and signs them, too, and this with his stories and a novel or two has made him a prosperous and distinguished gentleman. For two years after his marriage he lived on, almost as much of a recluse as he had before that time. But now he frequently drives into town at the side of his very beautiful wife, and while she purchases the necessities of the household, he remains outside in the carriage and passes the time of day with the good people of the village. Almost every day now, when the weather is fine, you can see him sitting on his porch or on a bench on the lawn watching a little child tumble about in a perfectly laudable effort to walk by itself. They say at Pleasant Harbor that it was the boy that brought Kerrigan out again into the sunshine and the company of his fellow men. But, as Fielding expresses it, as long as it was a child that took him out of the world for those miserable years it was only right, after all, that a child should lead him back again.

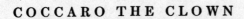

COCCARO THE CLOWN

COCCARO THE CLOWN

THE two men were seated in their new revolving
chairs before two new mahogany desks in the new
offices of the new theatrical firm of Henning & Conaway. Jacob Henning had spent the better part of his
fifty years in accumulating great sums of money, by
transforming rawhide into shoe leather; but now,
having reached his years of indiscretion, he had
planned to risk a portion of his fortune in the un-
certainties of the theatrical business.

Personally he was a large silent man, who was not
so keenly interested to make money in the new business as he was to view at close range the fleshpots
of Broadway, and to have the name of Henning
known beyond the somewhat narrow confines of the
leather trade. He had chosen Walter Conaway as his
partner, because in theatrical affairs the young man
had already shown some accomplishment and much

promise. Conaway had formerly been an advance
agent, and he therefore believed that silence was anything but golden.

"You may .be a very rich man, Mr. Henning,"
said the young manager. "I know money will buy
many things; but the hardest thing you ever tried to
buy in your life is a laugh."

Henning bit a little deeper into his cigar and
nodded his smooth moon face at his associate manager to continue.

"I can get you show girls and a working chorus
by opening that particularly dusty window over
there, that opens on Broadway, and then whistling
twice. You know how easy it was to buy a good book,
as far as plot goes, and if it isn't right we can buy a
couple of play carpenters for a shade under union
rates. There are as many song hits lying on the music
publishers' shelves on Twenty-eighth street as there
are tacks in a tack factory that's working night
shifts; but I tell you music and girls and a plot never
yet spelled success for a musical show on Broadway.
What we want are comedians, comedians that we
can loan the stage to for twenty minutes while the

girls are changing from an ostrich chorus to a birth of the poppy finale. We want two fellows who bring their own stuff with them and who carry it under their wigs and not on reversible cuffs, men who can ad lib. a scene if the lights go out, or the soprano wants to serve pink tea to her friends in the dressing room. And I tell you that kind are hard to get."

"Somebody gets them," Henning said slowly; "I've seen 'em. I hardly ever go to a theatre that some fellow on the stage doesn't make me laugh. If other people can buy comedians, then why can't we?"

"For two reasons," the metropolitan manager spoke glibly and with much decision. "All the good ones are tied up with their present managers; and they would be gagged, too, but you see that would interfere with their work. What we have got to do is to discover comedians—real comedians, latent geniuses, who work for thirty a week in low variety theatres."

"And then?" asked Henning.

"Then?" repeated the manager. "Then we fumigate them and their methods, tie them up with yards of red tape and eventually make them Broadway favorites, and ourselves, incidentally, successful managers."

"Do you know any of these diamonds in coal holes?" asked Henning a little sceptically.

The metropolitan manager looked out of the window on the yellow façade of the opera house on the other side of Broadway and then back to the Japanese parasol that screened the empty fireplace. Then he placed the tips of his fingers carefully together and looked Henning fairly in the eyes. "I think I do," he said deliberately. "That is why I have tried to make you understand the difficulty of the situation. Their names are Billy Danella and Coccaro the Clown; they're known as 'Coccaro and Danella.' An advance agent tipped them off to me last winter, and I looked them up the other night. They are working down on Eighth Avenue now, and the little one, Danella, is a knock out. He makes 'em scream all the time. Of course, he is very tough, and he will have to be sterilized for Broadway, but he was born comic and has naturally fallen into methods that legitimate actors take a lifetime to learn."

84

"And his partner?" asked Henning.

Conaway shook his head. "Just a feeder to Danella. He's a big, fine, athletic-looking chap, but he's not funny at all. He worked with Danella in the burlesque, but in the olio he did a rather neat turn with a woman. He makes up as a clown and has a trick dog, and she did a contortion specialty. I imagine they are circus people; and they could be of no possible use to us. However, if you say so, we'll go down there this evening and look them over."

That night the two men sat in the orchestra in the hot, dirty little theatre on Eighth Avenue. Through the fumes of ill-smelling tobacco smoke the low comedy work of Danella shone like a revolving light on a misty night. Every time he came on the stage, the packed, perspiring audience of many men and a few women laughed uproariously.

The silent Henning laughed and applauded the loudest of all. "He's immense!" he said, nudging Conaway. "I tell you he's great—just the fellow for the Mogul in our show!"

After the performance was over they stopped at the manager's office.

"Bob Jumel's my name, gentlemen," said the manager. "What can I do for you? Come in and take a seat." He was a short, thick-set man in shirt sleeves. A high silk hat was stuck on the back of his head, a half-smoked cigar hung down from heavy lips, and a great deal of cheap jewelry pinned to his waistcoat proved his membership in many secret orders.

"I wanted to ask you about Coccaro and Danella," said Conaway.

"I supposed that was it when I saw you in front. You're not the first that's been looking them over." He smiled genially at Conaway.

"Mr. Henning and I," said the Broadway manager, "are putting on a big extravaganza this summer, and we had a part we thought might suit Danella. Do you think you could let us have him? It would be a big chance. We are going to spend forty thousand dollars in real money, and we have all the time we want in the best theatre for a summer show on Broadway."

Jumel shifted his cigar to the other side of his mouth, put his feet on the desk in front of him, and for some moments gazed up at a dusty cobweb in the corner of the ceiling. "Of course, it's a good chance for the boys," he said. "I know that, and I know it's got to come some day; but you see they always work for me in the summer. I have a bit in a one-ring circus that plays through Western Pennsylvania and Ohio one-night stands, and the boys and Marzetta (that's Coccaro's wife you saw work with him in the first part) are about the best assets we've got. Both the boys clown for me with the circus, and they're great. I don't want to be no dog in the manger, but you know comedians are awful scarce. If they weren't, you wouldn't be looking for them down on Eighth Avenue."

"We're willing to pay a good bonus," suggested Conaway.

Jumel nodded. "Of course, I understand that. You'd have to pay them Broadway salaries, and I could get my bit out of that."

"As a matter of fact, Mr. Jumel," Conaway said, "we really could get along without Coccaro; it's the little fellow we want. What do you think?"

"No," said Jumel abruptly, "it wouldn't do at

all. Those boys have worked together for fifteen years. I know just how you feel about it; it's one of the oldest stories in the business; it's been the same with every team from Booth and Barrett to McIntyre and Heath. There's a weak end to every sketch; but you can't pry those kind of people apart with a crowbar. It's Coccaro and Danella or nothing. What would you give for the team?"

Conaway glanced at Henning, but the latter was apparently absorbed in a large fly-specked calendar over the manager's desk. "I don't want to haggle," said Conaway, "and I do want Danella. I'll give you two hundred a week for the team, and guarantee you eight weeks. If they don't make good, you can take them back and I'll make up the difference in salary."

"They'll make good all right," said Jumel. "I'll take two and a half."

Conaway again looked at his backer, and this time caught his eye. Henning shrugged his shoulders in assent.

"It's a pretty stiff price," Conaway said; "but if Mr. Henning is willing—" The three men rose and shook hands. "You had better bring them into the office to-morrow morning before lunch, and I'll have the contracts ready. Good-night, Mr. Jumel."

The four friends sat about a table in a back room of the saloon across the way from the theatre. There was Jumel still chewing the same unlit cigar; Jim Coccaro, broad and big, with the pink and white skin and the clear eye of the conditioned athlete; Billy Danella, small, pug nosed, ears that stood out at right angles to his blue, close-shaven face, a slit where his mouth should have been, and beady eyes that forever shifted and twinkled. The fourth member of the party was Marzetta the Contortionist, or, as she was known in her home life, Mrs. Jim Coccaro.

When Jumel had indulged in the most unusual occurrence of ordering a bottle of champagne, and after the waiter had left the room, he told the three members of his company of the wonderful fortune that had befallen them.

Danella's eyes blinked and shifted quickly from one to the other of the party. "I knew it would come!" he said, hitting the table fiercely with his closed fist. "It had to come! We've worked for it and we deserve it. They've been stealing my stuff for years; but I'll show 'em now—I'll show those Broadway robbers!"

Under the table Marzetta put her hand on her husband's knee and gently pressed it. They looked into each other's eyes and smiled with a thorough understanding.

To Danella this new prosperity meant not only money but a kind of fame, an acknowledgment of his comic powers, and from a public he had never even dared to hope that he would know. But to Coccaro and his wife it meant money, and money meant the power to break away from the theatre and the circus forever. Since the day of their marriage they had saved their pennies with the one thought before them of a farm all of their own where they would never again see chalk or grease paint or smell the damp sawdust under their feet. But until now the goal had seemed a very long way off. As soon as it was possible, they slipped away to their boarding house to talk over their happiness alone, and left Danella and Jumel still drinking and harking back to old scenes and bits of business which could be used effectively in the new play. It was early morning when the two men parted, Jumel silent, but Danella raving jubilantly over the sudden turn in his fortunes.

The next day at noon Coccaro, Danella, and Jumel met Conaway and Henning at the offices of the new management. The printed contracts, already filled in, lay on the desk, and Conaway, smiling, asked Danella if he would sign first.

The comedian took up the contract and, leaning leisurely against the desk, turned to the first page. "It says here," he said slowly, "that this contract is with the team Coccaro and Danella."

Conaway smiled again and nodded.

"That," continued Danella in the same deliberate tone, "is a mistake. The only contract I sign is for two hundred and fifty dollars for the services of Billy Danella. I have no partner—we quit last night."

Conaway turned toward Coccaro and Jumel, but the two men were looking at Danella in blank amazement. It was the clown who broke the silence.

"Why, Billy," he said very gently, "I don't understand. We've always signed as Coccaro and

91

Danella. You don't mean surely that—" He did not end the sentence, but put out his hand toward his old partner.

Danella folded his arms and leaned farther back against the desk. "Yes, that's what I mean," he said —"just that. For fifteen years I've supported you. I wrote your stuff, every line of it, and I taught you how to hand it to them. For fifteen years I have kept you and your wife alive. Everything you ate, every stitch of clothes on your backs, you owe to me. It was I who got the laughs, and just because we had been kids together I was easy and gave you half the money. Ask Jumel there, ask any stage hand who ever saw us work, how long you would have lasted without me. But that's over and done with now. You can sign in this company or you can go back to doing tricks with your poodle, Mr. Coccaro the Clown, and your wife can go on doing splits and drinking tumblers of water while she's twisted into a bow-knot; but you can't sign any more papers as Coccaro and Danella. I'm plain Billy Danella after this—Billy Danella, Comedian."

Henning, who had been sitting silent in a corner,

started forward, but his partner motioned him back. Conaway knew that Danella must be signed at any price. Throughout the long speech Coccaro had looked Danella evenly in the eyes, and now that his old partner had finished, he continued for some moments to do so still. At last he nodded as if in acceptance of the new arrangement.

"All right, Billy," he said—"all right, if that's the way you feel about it." He started to leave the room, but as he reached the door he turned once more to his former partner. "It's a long time we've been together—a long time is fifteen years, Billy."

Danella, with folded arms and drawn lips, looked stolidly at the wall before him. For a moment Coccaro hesitated. "It seems, gentlemen," he said at last, "that Danella and I can't do business any longer together. If you should still want me, Mr. Jumel knows where I stop in town. Good-day to you all."

During the next two days the two men signed separate contracts; Danella for the sum he demanded, and his former partner for just one-fifth of that amount. Indeed, if it had not been for the large heart of Henning and the strong appeal of Jumel,

Coccaro would have had to return to his old place in the circus. But if the life in town was a little easier for the clown and his wife, their finances had been scarcely bettered, and the goal of their wishes was just as far beyond their reach as ever.

When the production was completed and the last dress rehearsals were over, "The Mighty Mogul" company, a hundred strong, boarded a special train one bright Sunday afternoon in May and crept slowly out of the Grand Central Station. Its destination was a small New England town where the stage was large and where there was plenty of space for the carpenters and stage hands and electricians to become accustomed to the new material.

Unheralded, unknown, in the presence of a few New England citizens and half a dozen New York managers, "The Mighty Mogul" was finally born. After it was all over it seemed as if, besides the New England citizens and the New York managers, most of the good fairies must have been sitting about somewhere in the theatre, for they had certainly left their best gifts with the new monarch. The townspeople came in great numbers to see the play the following night; but long before that the news had reached the shady side of Broadway, and from Thirty-sixth Street to Forty-second Street the actors acclaimed it aloud, and just above the sidewalk the managers sat in their stuffy offices and chewed their cigars and wondered if it could be true.

It hardly seemed possible that Walter Conaway ("the boy manager," he was called) had built up a production that the wisest of the old guard of managers admitted was ten years ahead of its time. It had color and speed and novelty, at least so rumor said, and behind it all there was evident the money unlimited and the intelligence and the discretion of a new power. And there were wonderful tales, too, of a new comedian, one William Danella, who had a method all of his own, and who would make the first-night audience in New York sit up and take notice as it had not done in many seasons.

It was five o'clock the following Monday afternoon when Henning and Conaway left the theatre on Broadway and stood for a moment on the sidewalk looking up at the electric sign over the entrance.

Their work was over, and it was up to the actors and the head carpenter.

"Well, I guess it'll be all right," Henning said. "There's nothing else we can do, I suppose?"

Conaway laid his hand affectionately on his backer's arm. "Not a thing, Mr. Henning, not a thing; that is, except to step aside and see the limited pass. I told you we'd sneak away in silence and come back with bells on."

It was the call boy, who, while on his half-hour round, discovered that Danella was not in his dressing-room. A few minutes later the men and women who had already taken their seats in the theatre were surprised to see a man in his shirt sleeves, collarless, and with disheveled hair, run through the auditorium, and almost immediately run back again followed by two men in immaculate evening dress. Henning, Conaway, and the stage manager instinctively crossed the darkened stage in the direction of the entrance leading from the street. In the narrow hallway, just inside the stage door, they found Jumel dressed in ill-fitting, conspicuously new evening clothes, a great diamond in his shirt front. He was leaning dejectedly against the wall, his hands stuck deep in his pockets.

"Well," said Conaway, trying to keep himself in hand. "Do you think he may come yet?"

Jumel shook his head. "Hardly now, I should think. He always gets in by seven."

"When did you see him last?"

"I left him at a café across the street last night after the rehearsal."

"Don't you think we had better send up to his house?" suggested Henning.

"I've done that," answered Jumel; "but it's no use. He never goes home when he's like that."

Conaway turned white, and his teeth came sharply together. "So that's it, is it?"

Jumel nodded. "I guess that's it," he said.

"And so you sold us a gold brick; did you?"

Jumel did not answer.

"It seems to me, Jumel, we treated you fairly," Conaway snapped at him. "Why didn't you tell us?"

"How was I to know? He doesn't often go on a spree, and who would think he would fall down at a time like this? He was scared, that's all. The job was too big for him."

Henning stood solemnly by rolling an unlit cigar between his lips. "Just practically what does it mean?" he asked.

"It means we can't open," said Conaway. "It means we come in here with a big success and have to keep the house dark and risk forty thousand dollars, all on account of a variety actor."

"How about to-morrow?" asked Henning.

"That wouldn't do. There's a big syndicate opening and we'd get the second critics."

"It will have to be Wednesday, then?"

"Who knows?" answered Conaway despondently. "There's no telling when he will be back."

Henning took the cigar out of his mouth and licked the end carefully with his tongue. "I don't care so much about the money," he said slowly. "It really isn't that, but I have never had a failure in business before, and it hurts a good deal. Everything looked so well half an hour ago, too. It doesn't really seem fair, somehow. Of course, there's no one else we could put in; is there?"

Conaway and the stage manager looked at each other and shook their heads.

"There's been no time to get up understudies," Conaway explained. "A week later it would have been different."

"There's just one thing you can do," said Jumel, "and you've got an even chance to win out. Put Coccaro in the part."

Conaway looked at Jumel and laughed. "Jumel, I think you must be crazy. Coccaro never got a laugh in his life and you know it."

"Yes, he did," answered Jumel. "He's got 'em many times just like this, when Danella was off. He's no comedian, but he can give an imitation of the boy that would fool Danella's own mother; that is, if she kept her eyes shut."

"Oh, what's the use? He doesn't know the lines, anyhow," and Conaway turned away.

"I'll bet he does," said Jumel. "Didn't you notice how he stood at the wings always watching Danella. He's done that for years. I tell you it's a habit with him. You mayn't think he's as good as Danella, but the audience don't know."

99

Conaway turned to Henning. "Well," he said, "it's up to you, Mr. Henning. It looks like a long chance to me, even if he's up in the part."

Henning looked from one to the other of the faces of the three men. For a moment he hesitated. "I think I'd take a chance," he said.

"Who'll play Coccaro's part?" asked Conaway.

"That's all right," said the stage manager. "I can do that easy."

"All right," Conaway answered. "And now, Jumel, it's up to you."

As he finished the sentence Jumel started on a run for Coccaro's dressing-room.

Half an hour later Henning and Conaway were standing on the stage when Jumel, hot, perspiring, coatless, collarless, his suspenders tied about his waist, came out of the star's dressing-room.

"It's all right," he said—"it's all right. Marzetta has got Danella's part, and she'll stand on the O. P. side, and I'll take the book on the prompt side when Coccaro is on. You can ring in now. We'll be all ready, sure. And you two had better stay in front; it would make the boy nervous to have you back here." And Jumel dashed back again to the dressing-room.

Conaway pulled out his watch. "Eight-twenty," he said. "We'll practically ring up on time. It's pretty lucky; that is, if—" He smiled, and taking Henning by the arm led him off the stage and around back of the boxes to the front of the theatre.

During the performance the two men hung over the plush balustrade at the back of the parquet as if it had been the rail of a wrecked vessel.

"It don't seem possible," whispered Conaway. "It's the most wonderful imitation I ever saw."

Scene after scene Coccaro continued to read his lines, sing the songs, and do the dances. Compared to Danella, it was a little colorless, and the unction was not there; but, as Jumel said, "the audience didn't know." The play ran smoothly through its course, and the last curtain fell on a triumph for the new management. Henning and Conaway walked out to the lobby to receive the congratulations of their friends; but the word that they heard most often was the name of their new comedian Danella. The next morning the critics agreed that "The Mighty Mogul" had come to stay, and that one William Danella had secured a lasting place for himself in the brilliant firmament of Broadway stars.

Nothing was heard from Danella the next day, but late Wednesday evening Henning received a note from him. He and Conaway were sitting in the box office, happy and contented, and smiling at the empty ticket rack. Henning tossed the letter to his partner.

"All right," said Conaway when he had finished reading it; "but he might have given us a little more notice if he wants to go on to-night. I'll see him when he comes in."

"Will you let him play the part to-night?" asked Henning.

"Sure; that is, if he's all right. Why?"

Henning puffed slowly on his cigar. "Oh, I don't know. I suppose I'm new at the business, but it seems sort of hard on the other fellow to me. Don't you think we could keep him on?"

Conaway smiled and shook his head. "We've got Danella under contract for five years, and that means that he must create five parts. He'll have to give Coccaro half his salary for the two nights, any-how, and I don't think we ought to ask him to go back to his old part to-night. Besides, he doesn't seem to care to act—wants to be a farmer. Told me he was trying to buy a place up Connecticut way. Funny for a performer, eh? At that, I'm not very keen to tell him that Danella's going on to-night."

"Don't you mind," Henning said; "I think I'll see him myself."

He found Coccaro in the star's room. The clown was seated at his dressing table, slowly making up for the principal part. Henning sat down on a trunk in the corner of the room and cleared his throat.

"Mr. Coccaro," he began, "it seems Danella is coming back to-night and wants to go on."

Coccaro nodded and dropped the stick of grease paint he had been holding.

"We thought," Henning went on, "that you would like a night or two off, and so you needn't play your regular part to-night."

"If you don't mind," said Coccaro, "and it doesn't inconvenience you too much, I don't think I'll ever play that part again. I couldn't very well after—after what's happened. Jumel says I and my wife can go back to the circus."

For some moments Henning sat silent, swinging his short fat legs against the trunk. "It's a little hard to explain to you, Mr. Coccaro," he began. "I am not a man of words, and I find it difficult to say just what I mean."

Coccaro turned and smiled pleasantly at the manager. "Don't try, Mr. Henning," he said. "I know what you want to say."

"Perhaps you do and perhaps you don't. It wasn't the money, Mr. Coccaro. I have a great deal of that, more than I can spend. But it was my position. You saved me from appearing ridiculous to my old business friends, and your work that night turned disaster into a great success. I should like to do something for you that you and your wife would remember. Have you got a pen about here?"

"There's one over there on that table," he said. "I have been writing some autographs for Danella; but don't think I'll forget that first night, Mr. Henning. I'll remember that all my life."

Henning took a blank check from his pocket book,

filled it out, folded it, and handed it to Coccaro. "The receipts for the first two nights of the piece," he said, "were thirty-six hundred and two dollars and seventy-five cents. It seems to me, by all rights, they belong to you; and that'll go some distance, anyhow, toward that farm of yours."

Coccaro slowly rose to his feet protesting and held out his hand with the check in it.

"No, don't you be foolish," said Henning. "I've got a farm myself—I don't know how many hundred acres; but there's one little spot on it where I grow corn. I'll send you some of the seeds next October. I tell you it's the greatest corn in the world!" And Henning closed the door hurriedly behind him.

A few minutes later Danella came into the dressing-room: the two men nodded to each other and Danella took his place at the dressing table and began to make up.

It was after Coccaro had put on his clothes and was ready for the street that Danella broke the long silence. He spoke looking straight ahead into the mirror, and his voice sounded curiously even and almost without meaning

"I read in the papers that you made a great hit in the part. There's no good in my saying anything now; it's too late. But I'm much obliged. I'm sorry you've got to go back to that part."

Coccaro took his hat from a peg. "I'm not going back to the part," he said.

Danella continued to look at the mirror and to draw a stick of grease paint mechanically across his forehead. "Not going back?"

"No, and I'm not going back to the circus." Coccaro stopped on his way to the door and carefully traced out one of the patterns on the carpet with his walking stick. "No; I'm going to the farm. I've got it at last."

Danella dropped the grease paint, and without taking his eyes from the face in the mirror rested his chin between the palms of his hands. From outside there came the noise of many hurrying feet and the cry of the call boy, "Five minutes! Everybody on for the first act!"

Coccaro crossed over to the door, and then turned back with his hand on the knob. "According to the old plan, Bill, you were to have your room always at the farm. Well, if you ever get tired here and want to rest up a bit, you know the room is there waiting for you always. Marzetta and I wouldn't want any one else to have it."

For a moment he hesitated for a word from his old partner, but Danella did not answer him.

"Good-night," said Coccaro, and closed the door behind him. But when he had gone a few steps down the hallway, he returned and softly opening the door again, tiptoed across the room to where Danella lay on the dressing table his arms stretched in front of him, and his head resting between them. Coccaro touched him lightly on the shoulder. "That's all right; that's all right," he whispered. "You must get on your things now. They'll be ringing up on you in a minute. You mustn't take on so. I know how you feel. It's a long time we've been together, Billy, a long time."

"SEDGWICK"

"SEDGWICK"

WHEN Sedgwick first came to me, my friends said that I was a fool to take on a servant with such unsatisfactory references, and I suppose now, in a way, that they were right, but I am not quite sure. For three years I had had a man with the somewhat dazzling name of Tremaine, and a more consistent house-burglar I have never known; but he was consistent. So far as I know, he confined his peculations to jewelry, which I never wore, such as stick-pins and similar junk picked up at weddings and Christmases; black and white ties, suitable for evening wear, and Scotch whiskey, but always of inferior brand. I think Tremaine must have had a very common streak in him, for he never touched my really good wines or liquors, and for this I liked him. Every morning at eight o'clock he let himself into my apartment, laid out my clothes, and prepared my breakfast. At some time during the proceedings I would wake up and say: "How is it outside?" And if it was a bad, blustering, bitter cold day he would answer: "Fine, sir!" and lay out a thin suit, and if it was balmy and spring-like he would shake his head and say: "Pretty bad, sir!" and get out a heavy tweed and a fur overcoat. However, he was just as consistent about this as he was about his robberies; so I always went to the window, looked for myself, and had him make the necessary changes before he left the apartment.

This had been going on for nearly three years, when I was awakened one morning by the usual soft footfalls in my room, and I rubbed my eyes, cursed the fact that I was a workingman, and said: "How is it outside?" A strange voice replied: "It's very bad, sir—three inches of snow." I looked up and found an entirely unknown man brushing my derby hat.

"Who the devil are you?" said I.

"I'm Sedgwick. Tremaine is sick, and he sent me in his place."

"Is Tremaine very sick?" I asked.

The man slowly shook his head and answered in a most lugubrious voice: "Very sick, very sick, sir."

In two days it seemed as if Sedgwick had been with me always, and at the end of that time he confessed that Tremaine, whom he had but recently met at a servants' club, had never been ill at all, and had simply left me for a better place.

The only reference, therefore, that my new servant had was that of a thief and a man who had deceived me after three years of pretty good treatment. Of his past he told me nothing, and yet there was so much about him that I liked that I was loath to let him go. He was tall, thin, loose-jointed, lantern-jawed, by turns fierce and sad looking, and with that perfect knowledge of his business that only Englishmen of a certain class ever seem to acquire. He apparently took not the slightest interest in me or my affairs, but his honesty was beyond suspicion. However superior this particular kind of servant may hold himself to his master, I have never known one who did not have one weak spot—either a family affair or, more often, a former employer whose virtues he always took pleasure in talking about. But it was not so with Sedgwick. He never mentioned a former employer, a place where he had lived, nor an incident which touched on his past life. My friends delighted in him as a servant and a man of mystery, but always pretended to be fearful of leaving me alone with him. They insisted that he would one day probably cut my throat. Personally, I had no such fears, as he seemed to me a rather gentle, middle-aged person, and I had no doubt that concealed somewhere under his grim visage were a sympathetic soul and a heart of gold. To me he was like some thoroughbred bulldogs I have known, with their legs bowed, their eyes glazed, and their big jaws undershot and vicious, but jaws in times of peace that a child could put its hand between without fear of hurt.

Among the men who occasionally dropped in during the late afternoon, or the men and women friends who frequently supped at my apartment after the theatre, Sedgwick, apparently, had no favorites, and, what was still more unusual, he regarded the many photographs of the many women friends I had about my rooms with absolutely equal favor—or, perhaps, it was disfavor. In all my experience with servants. he was the only one who did not have an undisguised admiration for a particular photograph and insist on displaying it to its greatest possible advantage. But none of my beautiful friends seemed to appeal to Sedgwick, and he left them exactly as he had found them in the days of Tremaine or as I had since rearranged them according to my changing regard for the originals.

All of this was true for the first six months of his régime, and then somewhere (I think in the dusty depths of a music-rack) he discovered a photograph which I had forgotten as completely as I had the original. I found it one morning modestly displayed on a corner of the mantel over the fireplace in my sitting-room, and for a month in silence I watched it advance in prominence, until it stood side by side with the one photograph that made me regret that I still lived in bachelor apartments instead of a real home. It was a picture faded by time and soiled by ill-usage, never having risen to the dignity of a frame or the protecting care of a glass. When I had known

115

the original, years before, she was a blonde young woman, of Austrian birth, who, with a number of other girls, was studying music at Florence. They all lived in a cheap *pension* on the old side of the Arno, and were rather amusing and all perfectly secure in the belief that one day they would figure prominently among the world's greatest opera singers. This particular young blonde person I had known perhaps a little better than the others, but not much. We had climbed the hill to San Miniato and looked down on the glories of Florence; we had bicycled together through the shaded paths of the Cascine; side by side we had enjoyed the trolley ride to Fiesole, and lunched vis-à-vis at the Aurora. And one fine moonlight night we had stood together on the balcony of her *pension* and said *au revoir*, and when we went back to the little salon, which she shared with several other students, she had written some foolish words in French on a photograph of herself and given me the photograph. Since that day, to the best of my knowledge, I had never seen nor heard of the beautiful blonde Austrian girl, and I must confess that in the years that had elapsed my

116

interest in her had faded as rapidly and as surely as had her picture.

Not until the photograph had reached the highest point of conspicuousness to which it could possibly attain did I pretend to notice its sudden rise among my galaxy of international beauties.

"Sedgwick," I said one morning, "may I ask why you take so much interest in Miss Rose Parness?"

When Sedgwick was thoroughly embarrassed he took on a sort of gray putty color—blushing seemed to be an unknown accomplishment to him. On this occasion he turned particularly gray and cast a guilty glance toward the photograph.

"Cannot even a servant admire a great artist?" he asked. "You know, of course, who Miss Parness is now, sir?"

"Who—who is she?" I stammered. It was with some embarrassment I admitted my lack of knowledge, and the ignominy of my ignorance seemed to wellnigh overcome the valet.

"She is the great singer, Madame Marie Monteverde."

117

"Indeed!" said I, and I raised my eyebrows just as high as I could in polite astonishment. My ignorance in regard to grand opera and its singers was really shocking, but even I had heard of the beautiful and bewitching Madame Monteverde, who, I understood, was the present musical pet of New York.

"She is a great artist, sir"—and his glassy eyes fairly shone—"I think the greatest artist in all the world—but they have not yet given her the opportunity to prove it in America. Ah, sir, if you could hear her Carmen or her Mimi—Santuzza she has already done here—perhaps——"

"I fear not—I so seldom go to the opera. I knew Miss Rose Parness as a student in Florence."

"You were fortunate, sir. Is there anything else?"

In answer I shook my head, and he left me.

"So that is it," I said to myself, and grinned with pleasure at the fun I should have in telling my friends that Sedgwick, after all, was but human and had an undying affection for no less a person than the new popular soubrette of grand opera.

The discovery that Madame Monteverde and Rose Parness were one and the same person did not, I fear, arouse in me the interest which Sedgwick would have liked. As a matter of fact, the world of opera and the men and women who sing in it are objects of which I know little and care less. The singers and the musicians, their men and women secretaries, their accompanists and the little crowd of music-mad admirers, form a small coterie apart and talk a jargon of which I am wholly ignorant. I had often seen them lunching at a certain French restaurant, and it was amusing enough to watch them pose and strut and chatter together in a dozen different languages; but I was quite satisfied to be but a humble onlooker. Their start, as well as their whole lives, is, after all, founded on an accident of birth. God gives Brother James a husky frame, and he plows the fields for a living; God gives Brother William an extra wide throat, and Brother William makes a fortune every time he makes a moderate use of it. There is nothing traditional or hereditary about an opera singer—professionally, their family tree is a branchless trunk and their crest a larynx rampant.

Not, however, to appear too indifferent in the eyes of my servant, I allowed the photograph to remain where he had put it, and probably never should have thought of it again, had I not received news that my Cousin Muriel was about to pay her annual visit to the great city.

Of all the relatives and dear friends who drop in on me during the year, Cousin Muriel is the most welcome. All I have to do is to buy opera seats for her and the girl friend with whom she stays, and take them once or twice to the restaurant where the singers eat, so that they can see them at close range. This accomplished, she is perfectly happy, and returns to her bucolic home and tells her rustic friends that I am the ideal host and perfect cousin.

It so happened that while I was reading the letter announcing her early arrival, I happened to glance up and my eye caught sight of the photograph of Rose Parness. It gave me a wonderful inspiration, and I fairly chuckled aloud. I would give a supper party to the friend of my youthful days at Florence, and Cousin Muriel should meet and talk to a real opera singer. Among my friends there was no question that one Howard Danby was the logical choice to arrange the details. Danby was on the staff of an evening newspaper and one of my intimates for the half of every year. During these six months he reported baseball games and fires and an occasional criminal case; but when the opera season came along he assumed the title of Assistant Musical Editor, let his hair grow over his collar, shook out the camphor balls from his dress-suit, and spent his afternoons at tea with the lady opera singers and his late nights sitting about German restaurants, drinking beer with musical conductors who looked like French barbers, or the male singers who looked like Spanish bull-fighters, and low comedians from the Comédie Française. According to Danby, the last man I had seen him drinking beer with was always "the greatest tenor" or "the best barytone" or "the last word on Wagner," or, at least, "the husband of the coming only soprano," or "the accompanist of Puccini's own ideal of Madame Butterfly." What I considered operatic geese were all swans to Danby, and for six beautiful months in each year he fairly reveled in the smoke-laden atmosphere of garlic, high C's, and "My interpretation of the rôle."

I explained the situation to him, and he was de-

lighted with the commission. Of course, Madame
Monteverde must be seen first and reminded of the
old days at Florence, and, when her acceptance was
gained, Danby assured me that the rest would be
easy. A few days after I had first suggested the idea,
and just as Cousin Muriel was about to arrive, I received a letter from Danby, of which this is a copy:

It's all arranged for Thursday night of next week, at
your rooms. Madame Monteverde remembered you perfectly, and your little affair in the student days, but I think
I would call before Thursday, or leave a card, anyhow.
Very touchy, these big artists. I have got acceptances from
Merkel, who understudies the bass rôles; Cossi, a tenor,
who will set them crazy if he ever gets the chance; and
Count Morgenstern, an Austrian amateur pianist, *bon
vivant*, friend of all the singers, and I think a little *épris*,
just now, with your guest of honor. Besides Madame
Monteverde and your cousin, we will have Madame Zurla,
a great Senta—that is, if they do "The Flying Dutchman"
at all this season—Madame Czermak, a light contralto, but
very *chic* and pretty, and last, but not least, De Lisle, a
great favorite at the Opéra Comique in Paris. She is staying
here in the hope of getting a chance at "Thaïs" or some of
the undressed roles. I think, as a party, it is pretty hard to

beat. Of course, there are a few big names not on the list, but the average I consider high, and your cousin should get a typical glimpse of the great artists at their ease. *Au revoir.*

DANBY.

It seemed to me that there was a very serious lack of "big names" on the list, and that, with the exception of Madame Monteverde, my future guests had a good deal to accomplish before they could be ranked with the truly great. However, I was probably a prejudiced party, and the outlook loomed Bohemian enough to at least please Cousin Muriel.

The great night arrived at last. It was bitterly cold outside, a blustering wind whistled around the corners and the streets lay deep in snow, all of which made my apartment, with the blazing wood fires and warm, heavy hangings, seem all the more cosey and attractive. I had made a point of not telling Sedgwick who my guests were to be, and was not a little curious to see how he would behave in the actual presence of his divinity.

Madame Monteverde, in a wonderful spreading

pink hat and a sable coat, which with the collar turned up reached from her eyes to her feet, was the first to arrive. Sedgwick, I am quite sure, did not recognize her when she came in, as, after opening the door, he stood back of the singer, waiting to take her coat. The girl's cheeks were flushed scarlet with the cold, her eyes were shining brilliantly, and there was a smile on her lips as she turned toward him. When he saw her face, his hands, which were held out to take the coat, trembled and his arms dropped slowly to his sides. His sallow face turned grayer than I had ever seen it before, but what interested me the most was that the smile suddenly vanished from the face of Madame Monteverde. For a moment she looked him evenly in the eyes, and then the servant, bowing his head so low that it almost touched his breast, mechanically held out his hands and took the coat.

It was a curious incident, and I was glad that I had been its only witness. It seemed possible, too, that at last I was to learn something about the past of the melancholy Sedgwick.

I took Madame Monteverde into the library, presented her to Cousin Muriel, and returned to greet my other guests. They all arrived, looking very much the same—the men swathed in greatcoats and yards of silk muffled about their throats, and the women completely concealed in fur wraps. Danby assured me, between arrivals, that I should consider myself extremely lucky that they ever consented to come out on such a night. As a matter of fact, I had been wondering all along why they came at all—whether it was that they feared the criticisms of Danby's paper, or whether it was the prospect of a good supper. But once relieved of their outer garments, they seemed to be extremely glad to be where they were, and went about shaking hands—both hands at once—blowing kisses, clicking their heels, and bowing low to Cousin Muriel, and chattering their happy greetings like a lot of monkeys all at one time and in at least six different languages.

Madame Czermak—whose name I did not pronounce twice in the same way during the supper—looked rather *chic* in a very décolleté gown, and, as we had no formal singing, it did not matter how light her contralto voice really was; Madame Zurla appeared a ponderous person, who talked constantly of her happy summer home at Siena and of a son who was serving his year in the army; De Lisle was a dashing brunette, powdered quite white, who, when she was not chucking some one under the chin with a somewhat soiled lace fan, smoked a great many cigarettes between courses and after supper drank cup after cup of black coffee. In all ways she seemed worthy of the scandals that cluster about the little opera-house in Paris from which she came. Her conversation, if no more elevating than that of the other guests, was at least different, for while they talked only of what they sang, she never stopped telling me about her wardrobe, or rather the lack of it. The guest of honor—Madame Monteverde—I found much changed since the old days at Florence. Although still a girl in years, she was a woman now in the ways of the world; the unsought knowledge, the hard work, the grueling effort to overcome the obstacles in her way, had etched the telltale lines and shadows on the innocent, pretty face I once knew. Gracious as she was, there was a noticeable trace of the "professional artist" about her, and at times when she assumed an air of *diablerie* it was hard for me to believe that this was the girl I had known as a student in the little *pension* on the wrong side of the Arno. But yet, beneath it all, there was a certain sweet simplicity, a subtle appeal which must have carried across the footlights and which I could well understand had made her the idol that she was.

So far as the men were concerned, they all looked entirely different from each other, and yet, I am sure, possessed exactly the same insides. Merkel, the bass, had a tremendous frame, a face not unlike that of a horse, and a wonderful shock of tawny hair; Cossi was short and very stout, with glossy black ringlets, and talked as high as he sang; Count Morgenstern, the Austrian, was straight and blonde, with a little yellow mustache turned sharply up at the ends— apparently a common type of adventurer on the Continent, with much manner and no manners, a profound knowledge of the world and Who's Who; by profession an ex-army officer, and, I had heard, beyond his winnings at the gambling clubs, absolutely without means of support. Three more different-looking men could not well be imagined, and yet, I know, if their minds and souls and hearts could be analyzed, it would be found that all three contained precisely the same elements and in exactly the same proportions. They all wore baggy dress-suits, with tape sewed on wherever it was possible, frilled shirt fronts, and a great deal of unnecessary jewelry—principally turquoises. Merkel seemed to enjoy his supper much more than the others, but yet found ample time to say the most frothy, inane things in a sepulchral voice to the fascinating De Lisle, while Cossi, who did not really seem to care to whom he talked, or what he said, chatted merrily in his piping voice to the ponderous and motherly Madame Zurla. Morgenstern divided his time between Cousin Muriel and the unpronounceable Czermak; but it easily could be seen that Danby was right, and such mind and heart as the blonde ex-officer had were the sole property of Madame Monteverde.

If unceasing chatter, hilarious laughter, snatches of light song startlingly well sung, cleared plates, rows of emptied bottles on the sideboard, constitute a successful supper party, then, I think, my supper party to Madame Monteverde for Cousin Muriel was a success. Of the culinary part of the entertain-

ment I felt justly proud, and Sedgwick, once recovered from his first shock of meeting with his divinity,
served the suppor superbly. Of one fact I am quite
certain; by the time the coffee was brought on I had
as my guests the greatest of all great opera singers of
all the world, and the only reason this fact was not
known universally, was because all impresarios had
wooden heads. I am sure of this, because my guests
told me the facts over and over again. I really think
Madame Monteverde enjoyed talking over the old
days at Florence, and Cousin Muriel's eyes fairly
glistened as she leaned well over the table, fearing
she would miss some pearl of thought, and at the
same time inhaling great draughts of cigarette smoke
and patchouli into her pure pink lungs, in the honest
belief that it was artistic atmosphere. When Sedgwick had served the coffee and left the tray of cordials
on the table, he retired to the adjoining room, to
await the departure of my guests. The door had no
sooner closed behind his back than Madame Monteverde asked what I knew about my servant and
how he had happened to come to me. After the little
incident I had witnessed in the hallway, I cannot

say that her somewhat pointed question surprised me.

"As a matter of fact," I said, "I really know nothing. He is what you, in your profession, would call an 'understudy.' He came to me almost a year since to take temporarily the place of a man I used to have, and he has been with me ever since. The only thing I know about him is that his one interest in life seems to be you. What do you know?"

Madame Monteverde smiled, shrugged her pretty shoulders, and taking a cigarette from the table, rolled it between her thumb and forefinger. "I never really met him—strictly speaking—but once before," she said slowly, "and on that occasion I had him thrown into jail." The buzzing about the table suddenly ceased, and my guests sat forward on their chairs. For the moment Madame Monteverde had their undivided attention.

"Funny!" said Morgenstern, with a sort of proprietary air, "I never heard of that. Was he a robber?"

The singer shook her head. "Not at all. As a matter of fact, it was all my fault; he was quite innocent. It was two seasons ago, when I was singing at

"It was two seasons ago, when I was singing at Monte Carlo."

Monte Carlo. Every day I used to receive a letter from an unknown admirer; at first he was simply fulsomely flattering, and then he began threatening me because I refused to answer his letters, and finally he said he was going to shoot me. We called in the police, and the only man I could suggest as the possible writer of the letters was this servant of yours. Almost ever since I have been known at all he has followed me. When I first went to sing at Milan, he was there, and afterward I saw him at Paris, and later at London, when I sang at Covent Garden. Nearly every night I would find him at the stage door, but he was very quiet—never came near me— just stood in the crowd, if there was a crowd, and gazed at me with those big, glassy eyes of his. And on bad, rainy nights, when the streets were deserted, there he would be, pretending that it was not I he was waiting for. But goodness! there was no mistaking why he was there. Really, he used to look at me sometimes in a sort of hungry way, and then I never felt safe until they had closed the door of my carriage. And then sometimes I thought I would speak to him, because he seemed so miserable, and his clothes were often very poor and worn, and he looked starved and so in need of a kind word—or, perhaps, a little help."

Little Cossi leaned his elbows on the table, and breathing on his monocle, rubbed it with his silk handkerchief. "And yet you had him put in jail!" he piped in his high voice.

Madame Monteverde looked up and smiled at the pudgy little tenor. "Yes, indirectly I had him put in jail. I told the police how he had followed me from city to city, and they, of course, were quite sure that he was the man. The same day I got a note from my admirer, saying I must meet him that night back of the Casino, after the rooms had closed. It was arranged that I should start for the rendezvous, but that the police should, of course, always be near me. They shadowed this man of yours during the evening, and when they saw him leave the rooms after I did, and apparently follow me, they arrested him. Just as they were busy doing this, the real man—who was probably a perfectly harmless crank—jumped up from behind a hedge and ran down the hill through the gardens. One of the policemen followed, but lost him in the crowd at the railway station."

"And then!" Cousin Muriel gasped.

"Then—well, oh, then, the toy policemen had to put somebody in jail, so they locked up this poor soul for the night. There was nothing against him, and naturally, they had to let him go the next morning. I felt terribly about it, but I only saw him once afterward."

"Did you speak to him?" I asked.

Madame Monteverde shrugged her pretty shoulders. "I was walking down the hill to Monaco a few days later, and met him coming up. You remember there is only one sidewalk, and that is rather narrow. I stopped, but the moment he saw I recognized him and was going to speak, he stepped into the street and stood with his hand to his cap at a sort of salute. So I simply bowed and walked on. That is the last time I saw him until to-night."

Madame Monteverde drew her scarlet lips into a straight line and threw the unlit cigarette she had been holding back on the table. "And, you know, the curious thing about it all is," she said, "that I believe he is absolutely sane."

The singer glanced at a little diamond watch she wore on her corsage, and rose from the table.

"I don't want to break up the party," she added, "but it's much later than I thought."

The rest of the guests rose, too, and we went into the library, where Sedgwick had brought the coats and wraps.

With many effusive thanks and protestations of undying regard, the party made their adieux. I was much pleased that my little supper had been a success and the evening had passed so happily, and I was glad, too, to have heard something of my melancholy servant. Cousin Muriel and the other women, with the exception of Madame Monteverde, had put on their furs and gone out into the hallway. Sedgwick had retired to the far end of the room and was standing by the window; the rest of us were ranged about Madame Monteverde, watching Count Morgenstern put on her wrap. I think the fool must have been a little befuddled, for after he had once put the heavy fur mantle about her, he lowered one corner of it and deliberately kissed her on the bare shoulder. Even in the dimly-lit room it was easy to see the blood rush to the girl's face. I looked back of me and saw Sedgwick bending almost double and ready to spring. It was too late to do more than jump in between him and Morgenstern, and the next moment the servant came crashing into us. With a cry, Madame Monteverde ran into the hallway and slammed the door behind her. Sedgwick slowly rose to his feet and stood staring at Morgenstern, his long arms and big hands hanging before him, looking more like a huge gorilla than a man. At the moment I would not have given a farthing for the life of Morgenstern. Twice Sedgwick tried to speak, but the words died in his throat, and then suddenly he seemed to find his voice, and he cried out:

"You cur! You blackguard! You've insulted my child—my own child, do you hear, and you've got to 'answer to me—to me!"

Morgenstern slowly stepped back toward the wall, and Merkel and Cossi closed in in front of him. I grabbed Danby by the arm and pushed him toward the door.

"Start those women home!" I said. "You'd better look out for Monteverde, and, for the love of Heaven, don't tell her what this man said!"

135

Sedgwick backed a few feet away from the little group of foreigners, but not for one moment did he take his eyes from the white face of Morgenstern. I knew that this time he would reach his man, and I stood aside and watched him. With his left arm he knocked over Merkel and Cossi as if they had been a couple of wooden tenpins, and almost at the same moment whipped his big right hand across Morgenstern's face, and raised a welt that looked as if the man's forehead had been cut with a wire thong. For a moment the lithe, straight figure of the Austrian wavered, and then crumpled up and fell back into a cabinet filled with glass. Cossi and Merkel stooped over to see just how badly their friend was hurt, and Morgenstern lay there among the broken glassware, moaning and whining like a starved cat.

I looked at Sedgwick and nodded toward the far end of the room. He shrugged his heavy shoulders, and, with a last look at Morgenstern, moved away.

With the help of the two singers, I dragged the Austrian into my bedroom, bound up his wound as best I could, and packed him off in a cab to his hotel, where I telephoned to have a doctor waiting for him.

I returned to the apartment and found Sedgwick in the library, where I had left him. He had pulled back the curtains and stood looking out on the snow-covered streets. I shut the door with a snap, and he slowly turned his big ungainly frame toward me.

"You look pretty white," I said. "You'd better take a drink of something."

"I am discharged?" he asked.

"Yes, you are discharged."

The man bowed, walked over to a sideboard, and gulped down a big drink of neat brandy. I sat down at my desk and lit a cigar.

"Do you know how much I owe you?" I asked.

He put up his hand, as if by way of protest, and slowly shook his head. The fire had gone as quickly as it had come, and left only the gray face and the meaningless eyes.

"I don't suppose there is anything you want to say?" I asked, and turned toward the desk.

"Yes, there is something I should like to say, now I am no longer in your service."

I turned back again to the putty-colored face. "Won't you sit down?"

137

My ex-valet shook his head. "No, I'd rather stand
—it won't take long. I'm going to tell you this, because you were the only gentleman who was willing
to take a chance with me. You don't know the kind
of jobs a man is reduced to when he has no references, and is up against it and can't stay put in one
place! You took me up and pretty near made a man
of me. This is the first home I have seen in a long
time."

"That is hardly a reason," I suggested, "for beating my guests into pulp."

He paid no heed to my remark, but walked over to
where I sat and rested one of his big hands on the
desk and looked down at me. He began the story in
a perfectly even voice, without any apparent animus
or feeling of any kind toward any one:

"I went to Vienna when I was a very young man.
My father was a clergyman in Lincolnshire, with six
children, and I was put to work in the bank in the
little town where we lived, and I couldn't stand the
sight of so much money. I was very young, and weak,
too, and when I took the money I got away to Vienna.

138

It really was not very much money, and I heard afterward my father fixed it up somehow; and for that, and I suppose to avoid scandal at the bank, they let me stay where I was. I had a good education and spoke several languages, and, with the money I had, I got along pretty well and made some good friends. One of these kept a big store and was quite rich. I fell in love with his daughter and she cared for me, but the father—old Parness—did not like me as a son-in-law. So we ran away and got married, and her family shut their door against her——"

For a few moments Sedgwick hesitated and opened and closed the hand that lay on the desk, and, while his eyes seemed to be looking into mine, I knew that they were looking through me to a time many years past.

"For one year," he began again, "we were very happy—both of us very happy. It was hard on her because we were poor and she had always had everything. I got a job as a clerk in a hotel, where I could interpret for the tourists. And then our girl—our little girl Rosa—was born, and what should have been our greatest happiness was the end of it all. Her family offered to take my wife back if she would leave me, and she was very ill and I had so little to offer her and to Rosa—not even a decent name—for the story of the bank had already come back to us several times. I believe—I am sure now—that my wife would have in time returned to me, but—but she did not live so very long after that. And then her family came with an offer to adopt Rosa and educate her and to do everything that money could do to make her happy and protect her, and, in face of all this, I could offer her but a home in the hotel where I was an under-clerk——"

The man hesitated and looked down at me, as if asking permission to go on, so I nodded and he went on:

"And although I could not see her or speak to her, I always knew something of what she was doing. I heard of her going to Florence, and then, after her success at Milan, everything was quite different, because she belonged to the world and I could go to see her like every one else. That has been my life, sir, to follow when I could and sit up in the gallery

Morgenstern lay there among the broken glassware.

the nights she sang, and listen to her and to see her
and to hear the crowds applaud and sometimes cheer
her, and bring her out before the curtain again and
again. I tell you, they love her—it's not only the wonderful voice, but it's the girl they love. And very
often I used to wait at the stage-door and in front of
her hotel and see her come out, dressed up as she
was to-night at supper, and watch her get into her
carriage." And then, for the first time, I saw Sedgwick's features relax into what on any other face
would have been a smile.

"And do you know, sir," he said, "that one night
at Monte Carlo they had me arrested and put me in
jail for following her! They thought I meant harm to
Rosa—to my own child!"

"And Morgenstern?" I asked.

The smile faded from his face and he rubbed his
coat-sleeve slowly across his forehead.

"I don't know," he said, "I don't know—these
women have so little sense. He has been following her
for two years now; he is a blackguard, trying to marry
her for her money—an adventurer—you could tell
that. I know that he was thrown out of a club in

Paris for turning the king too often at *écarté*. I tell you——"

The man suddenly stopped talking, and a curious, confused look came into his eyes.

"My God!" he whispered, "I never thought of that. Do you think they would tell her?"

"Tell her?" I repeated.

"Yes, tell her what I said when I lost my head there—tell her that I said she was my own child! Do you know what that means—do you know that I can never go near her or let her see me again?" He grasped my arm in his big hand, and stared into my eyes. "Tell me," he whispered, "will they tell her?"

"From the way I heard them talk to-night," I said, "I believe that crowd would tell anything."

Sedgwick let go the grip on my arm and walked slowly back to the window. For a few moments he stood with his big back silhouetted against the long frosted panes of glass, and then he turned again and faced the room.

"But after all," he said, "I can still see her on the stage. I can see her and hear her, and when they cheer her, and she comes out and bows and smiles at them, and they shout and throw their bouquets to her, I can say to myself that that is my child—after all I have done something. For that is something, sir, don't you think, to give a great singer to the world?"

"Yes," I said, "much more than most of us do. But, after all, what if they should tell her? Why not let me tell her?"

The man looked at me as if he could not quite understand the meaning of my words. "Tell her!" he repeated, "tell Madame Marie Monteverde that her father is a broken-down servant! Ask her to recognize me as I am after more than twenty years!" He spread out the palms of his hands toward me and looked down at his own gaunt, ungainly frame. "Not that," he said, and it seemed as if he was talking only to himself. "I must be getting away now. I'm sorry to go, but she does not leave for Paris before the spring, and by then——"

The electric bell at my front door rang out through the silent rooms, and so shrill and unexpected was it at that hour that I unconsciously started to my feet. I looked at Sedgwick and found him with his arms hanging at his side, the palms still held outward, and his eyes staring straight ahead of him. I went out into the hallway and opened the front door. In the dimly lit corridor I saw my friend Danby, and back of him the figure of Madame Monteverde, wrapped in her fur coat and her face shaded by the big pink hat.

For a moment no one spoke, and then the girl came toward me.

"Is—is he—is my father still here?" she asked.

I nodded toward the library, and she passed me and went in, and I watched her close the door softly behind her.

Then Danby and I sat down on the bench in the hallway and waited.

A MODERN CLEOPATRA

A MODERN CLEOPATRA

IF Escott had planned his own downfall, he would not have had it otherwise. His failure was absolute and complete, and until the last moment he had lived as he had always lived.

The young man had spent the morning and the greater part of the afternoon in the little glass office of his broker. "Of course," said his financial adviser, "we are willing to increase your margins for your own sake, and the sake of your father, who was a good client, but I fear that we could not help you sufficiently to beat out the present market. Besides, we but followed your instructions. The fault, you must admit, was yours, not ours. Sell now and the statement shows you owe us nothing. A few days, a few hours, and you may be hampered with a debt which it will take you years to pay back."

Escott got up and with much deliberation pulled on his gloves.

"That seems easy," he said. "Then I owe you nothing?"

"Nothing," echoed the broker. "We will call your account balanced, and let me assure you that you have acted wisely. I hope that some day you will build up another fortune as great as your father's, and once more become one of our valued clients."

Escott smiled and ran lightly down the steps. He gave the address of his lawyer to the cabman and, the smile still playing about his lips, fell back into the deep cushions of the hansom. The young man felt as if a great weight suddenly had been lifted from his mind: the struggle was over and now he knew the worst. For months he had hung on with a terrible tenacity to the hope of building up a new fortune on the small remnants of his patrimony. During this time he had not changed his mode of life one iota, and when the end seemed to be approaching he had placed his little all on one coup which, if successful, might have saved him. But the coup was not successful. He had failed, but he owed no one a farthing.

His life to the present had been laid along a smooth and shaded pathway; on either side were pleasant pastures in which he had roamed at will with no heed of the future. Above the shade-trees that lined his path the sun had forever seemed to shine, and its rays glinted through the boughs and had lighted him on his joyous way. But now he had come to a great stone wall, sheering high above him; the shadow of warning it had thrown in his path had been unheeded, and he was face to face with the rocks and mortar. He stood before it impotently. Good health alone was his; his life had taught him no means of overcoming the obstacle that faced him.

The cab stopped before his lawyer's door, but the office was closed. After all, it mattered but little. He knew that there was nothing owing to him, and the interview could have ended only in harsh words and a beggarly loan, and at heart he was glad to avoid both one and the other.

Not until he had reached his own warmly lighted rooms did he seriously consider, or acknowledge to himself that a great change had come into his life, and that a decision of serious import must be reached, and at once. For a moment he tried to avoid the struggle that was inevitable, and lay back in an easy-chair listening to his servant moving quietly about the ad-joining room. And then, as if to arouse himself, he stood up and threw the cigar he had been smoking into the hearth. Whatever there was to do must be done alone; he wished no one to be a partner in his ignominy.

He called his servant and the man appeared at the doorway.

"Yes," he said, "I think you had better put out my evening things, and after I go out pack up all my clothes. I am going away. Come to-morrow and make the rooms ready for the agent. Put the photographs in the trunks, and you had better take any of the bric-à-brac that is mine for yourself."

"Thank you, sir," said the servant. "Am I to go with you?"

"No, I think not. I'm afraid I shall not need you for the present. I am sorry that I could not give you more time to look about for another place."

Escott took out his pocketbook, and gave the man the last bills it held.

"There are your wages for two weeks," he said. "That is usual, is it not?"

The man bowed and left the room, shutting the door behind him. "And now," said Escott, half aloud, "where the devil am I to go? Leave these rooms I certainly must. If I stay in New York I shall have to take a clerkship—that is, if I can get one— and that probably means a refined boarding-house at best."

And then there came over him an awful dread of the life that he must lead in the city where, at least in his own set, he had once been of some import. He knew that he was no longer a part of it—only a miserable outsider. With it all came a great love for his life of the past, and the material side of it rose up before him and seemed doubly attractive to him now that it was beyond his grasp. To it all there seemed but one answer. He must leave the town and the people he loved, and must begin again where there was nothing to remind him of all the happiness that he had known and that was to be his no longer.

"Thank God," he said, "there is still time to leave it with honor!" He threw himself into a chair, and burying his head in his hands thought of the men he had known, whom he had seen fail as he had failed,

and who had lacked the strength to fly away from it
all. Some of them had become secretaries to rich
friends, sometimes in their offices, sometimes in their
homes, but always with salaries out of all proportion
to their worth. Some spent their lives as guests in their
friends' houses, wandering from place to place, living
in the hope that the next mail would bring them a
letter offering a bed and board for the following week.
It mattered not whether it was on a yacht or a special
train or only a country house—it meant food and
drink, a week more of ease, a week less of honest
work. And then there were certain men he knew at
the clubs. No one was quite sure how they even paid
their dues, but they made many wagers and were
known to win often at cards—people seemed to forget the occasional losses till the final breaking up and
the sudden disappearance came. And then there
were the men who sold themselves and their father's
name and were married to the highest bidder.

No, he would not be one of these. "Broke," he
said to himself, "but not a blackguard."

He walked across the room, and raising the window, looked down on the black city with its myriad of

yellow lights. The noise of the streets rose in a great wave, and as he held tightly to the window-frame, the towers and church steeples seemed to waver slightly, and the high buildings to rock slowly on their foundations, and all seemed to be moving toward him. "My God," he muttered, "how I love it."

An hour later Escott had fully realized the novelty and extreme seriousness of his position. It was most contradictory, and the situation was not without humor even in the eyes of the chief actor in this modern tragedy. He sat in a luxurious room, dressed as well as the best English tailor and valet could make him; his assets, an extensive wardrobe, the tickets for a box at a music hall for that night, a dollar bill and a few silver coins. There were two courses open to him. One was to sell the luxurious wardrobe, pawn the little jewelry he owned, and with the proceeds leave New York to begin a new life far from the world he knew and liked so well and where he was equally well known and equally liked. The idea of beginning again in New York was not worthy of consideration. The other alternative was made possible by an excellent credit. It had been done before, and was being done every day. With a few loans easily contracted from his immediate friends, and a good run of credit at the clubs, the restaurants and the shops where he was known, he could live in luxury for weeks, even months. He had known some men do it for years. In the meantime something might turn up. If it didn't—well! he could then leave town and begin his new workaday life. There would be some unpleasant things said about him, but after all, it would soon be forgotten, and no doubt he would one day return and pay back the money and resume his old position, or nearly the same position. The world, on the whole, he inclined to believe, was generous to young men who had temporarily fallen by the wayside.

The thought loomed before him a great temptation, and in his heart he had a terrible desire for one last round of pleasure before he left this material world which always had been so extremely kind to him.

Whatever he did, he felt must be done at once. He knew that he should turn his back on it all and seek

154

honor in flight; it was really the only course, and after
the first step the rest would be easy. But he feared to
take the first step. It was nearly dinner-time, he
was rather hungry, and he could sell nothing before
the next morning: he must either dine on the little
money he had or open an account at a restaurant.
There was the first hurdle rising directly in front of
him, and he could take it as a thoroughbred hunter
should or he could shy at it like a dog. The young
man buttoned his coat tightly about him, and set out
to look for his first cheap dinner. It was nearing seven
o'clock when he turned into the avenue. In the half
dozen blocks he walked he passed as many doors
where he could have entered and been sure of a
hearty welcome and a good dinner, but there was to
be no turning aside, no chance for a change of decision on the morrow. The solemn doors of his friends'
houses tempted him but little, and so he passed them
by until it occurred to him that the avenue was not
the place to look for restaurants where they served
dinners for a dollar. He turned down Thirty-fourth
Street and in a few minutes found himself on Broadway. The street, with its thousands of white and

yellow lights, was crowded with men and women returning from their work, and he regarded them with a new interest and wondered how he should play their part. They certainly seemed a happy, contented lot. A newsboy ran in front of him and thrust an evening paper into his hand. Escott took the paper mechanically, and while he was looking for his change asked the boy how much he made on each paper and how many he sold a day.

"Half a cent on each copy," he repeated after the boy, "and you sell perhaps thirty on a good day." He told the boy to keep the change, and went on, whistling softly to himself.

He had gone but a short distance farther when he heard a woman's voice calling him by name, and then a hansom drew up suddenly at the curb and a girl alighted, and without paying him much heed gave the driver some directions about meeting her later in the evening.

Miss Stella Brunelle had never before inspired any particular interest in Escott, and she certainly did not do so at this moment when his thoughts were distinctly of a serious nature. He had frequently watched her with pleasure from a box at one of the music-halls, and she had appeared to him as part of a bright and pleasing picture. Her physical attractions on and off the stage were easily evident, but as to her mental powers or views of life in general he had chosen to remain in ignorance. He had known Miss Stella Brunelle for some time, as he had known many other women of the stage, and on several occasions she had been his guest at supper-parties after the play.

"I like Stella Brunelle," he had explained once, "because to my mind she fills the youthful ideal of what a stage beauty really should be, and I always ask her to supper when I have a college man or a friend from the country stopping with me. Presumably she does eat eggs and drink coffee for her breakfast, but I always somehow imagine her confronted by hot birds and a frosted wine-cooler at her feet. My college and bucolic friends all delight in her, but personally I don't know that we have ever exchanged five words."

When Miss Brunelle had dismissed her hansom, she turned to Escott with a show of much enthusiasm and apparent real delight at the meeting.

"Well, I am glad," she said. "I was that lonesome at home that I simply couldn't eat by myself, so I came downtown in the hope of finding some one to dine with. Now, don't tell me you have an engagement. If you have, send them a wire. I must have dinner with somebody."

Escott threw away his cigarette, and looked down into Miss Brunelle's large, appealing eyes.

"No," he said, meditatively, "I'm not dining with any one. Quite alone, in fact." He hesitated for a moment and took a cursory inventory of Miss Brunelle's furs and her glistening white gloves.

"I was thinking," he said, "of trying one of those Sixth Avenue tables-d'hôte. They do say you get the most remarkable dinner for fifty cents. Have you ever tried one?"

"I certainly have," answered Miss Brunelle, "and I can't see them with field-glasses. Tables-d'hôte and beefsteak parties are all right in a big crowd on Saturday nights, but this is only Tuesday."

"So it is," he answered, "only Tuesday, as you say. Still, I rather like the idea of just you and me dining alone at a table-d'hôte. You know they throw in

wine and coffee, and olives and—and salted almonds
for all I know."

"But why?" said Miss Brunelle, a little impa-
tiently. "Here we are at the very door of a fine
palm-room. Why go farther?"

"Why, yes; why, of course," he said. "Let's go in
here."

For just a moment he stopped at the door. How
absurd it all was, to be sure—only the cost of the
dinner. He could pay the next morning, and yet he
could not help the feeling that he had been a little
weak, for in a way he had broken the promise he had
made to himself and the cause was hardly a worthy
one.

They walked down the long room under the
palms, the mirrors reflecting their figures as they
passed. Escott knew half the people at the tables and
nodded to them as he followed the maître d'hôtel to
the end of the restaurant. The girl stopped to speak
to some of her friends, but Escott seemed to wish to
avoid them as much as it was possible, and did not
halt until he had reached his own table.

There certainly was a charm about it all—the low

music, the dull marbles and the old-gold pillars, and the bright dresses of the women half hidden by the palms, and Miss Brunelle sitting opposite to him at the little table with its snowy linen and heavy silver and fine glass. As she slowly drew off her gloves, he looked up curiously into her face, shaded by the dull light of the little pink table-lamp. She seemed to him to have a great deal of beauty at that moment.

"And now," she said, briskly, "what is it to be?"

"What do you think?" he asked.

"Well, you know I'm out of that bit in the first of the act, and don't come until near the end, so I have plenty of time. My idea about a dinner," she ran on, "is to have nothing that is ready or inexpensive, and simplicity only as regards length."

"I should say that meant," he said, "caviare, terrapin, duck with salad, and café extra. What do you think?"

"Yes," she said slowly, "and let us compromise on something fairly dry."

The dinner ordered, Miss Brunelle settled back into her chair and smiled contentedly across the table.

160

"Billy," she said,—"you don't mind me calling you Billy—everybody does. What are you going to call me?"

"Oh, I don't know—Miss Fate, I think, might be an appropriate name."

"Why Miss Fate?" she asked. "Is that a part in a play?"

"Yes," he said, "it's a character part in a tragedy called 'Life.'"

"Really, but I wouldn't look so serious about it if I were you, and for heaven's sake don't look me all over like that. Is there anything the matter with my collar?" Miss Brunelle turned and gazed at herself in the mirror.

"It wasn't your collar so much as your face that interested me," he said. "They say that every Antony has his Cleopatra, but I somehow never imagined you as mine. But we can never tell, can we?"

"Cleopatra," repeated Miss Brunelle—"I saw Mrs. Potter in the part when I was a kid. I forget Antony. What did he do?"

"Antony? Well—he had a big, fine thing to do,

and he started out to do it all right and then he met Cleopatra, and he ran away."

"What, ran away from the lady?" said Miss Brunelle. "How brusque!"

"No, he ran away from the fine thing."

"All on account of the lady?" asked the soubrette. "Times haven't changed much, have they?" and she glanced significantly around the restaurant.

"Thank heaven, here's the caviare," she added. "And Cleopatra—she let him run away from the stunt?"

"Oh, yes," he said; "times haven't changed much in that respect either, do you think?"

"Well, now," said Miss Brunelle, "I don't know. There was Johnny Andrews. Did you know him? He went broke. Races, I think—and he side-stepped —never so much as said good-by. A girl sent him away. I'll never forget the night he got back; he walked into the box and Elsie fainted. Well, the whole show stopped, and old Gessler, that led the orchestra and never was known to speak to any one, stood up and bowed to him." Miss Brunelle picked up a piece of bread and broke it reflectively. "I guess that was the gayest supper I ever attended."

Escott leaned back in his chair and looked curiously into the girl's face.

"Miss Brunelle," he said, "you are very interesting to me because you are the ideal of a certain type." The girl smiled doubtfully. "I should like your opinion in a certain matter," he went on very slowly, "because I know that you are quite honest. Now suppose a man you knew, a man like myself, who is believed to have plenty of money, should wake up some day and find himself ruined. Quite ruined—I mean literally without a penny. You wouldn't say to him, 'Go away,' would you? It seems to me you would say: 'Better stay here; a few more dinners, a few more suppers, what matter the cost in the future? Here there's life and pleasure; we will smile at you, and we will make you laugh. After all, our interest ends with the liqueurs. The bill is paid by somebody, some time.' That is what you would say, wouldn't you?"

He was speaking with great earnestness, and, leaning far over the table, looked anxiously into the

163

girl's face as if her answer was of much moment to him. "Look at the men about us," he went on. "What do you know of them? To-day they are rich, because they are spending their money like Indian princes. But how is it to-morrow? How many men have you and I seen here fail miserably with debts everywhere? Do we care? We have eaten with them, drunk with them and laughed with them. Does it matter after all from where the money comes? We have paid our debt in our presence and in our poor jokes. We owe them nothing."

Miss Brunelle put down her fork and looked casually over the different men and women sitting near her. "Well," she said, "now there's—but that's personal. I think perhaps we would all act differently. Some of our friends here to-night should be in jail and some have a fair right to be at large. The trouble is that when we are making two hundred a week we forget the day when we carried a spear. It's really wonderful how quickly you can educate yourself from a piece of bacon to a partridge breast. I don't suppose there is hardly a woman here to-night that hasn't done a sketch in a ten-twenty-and-thirty show, and now look at us. Why, I remember the days when they used to give out the parts, I didn't care whether I had one line or was the whole show, and I can remember when I used to lend the other girls my rouge and hare's-foot and help pack the star's trunk for her. These long engagements in New York and this taxicab life do make one a little selfish, I guess. As you say, Billy, I suppose we do rather come to regard these things as our rights, and I don't imagine we do think much of when or how it all comes. If you had ever done a season of one-night stands you would know what a good New York engagement means. Heavens, how I hate the road; this is the real thing. No trains and early calls and lunch-counter dinners for me again. Eat, drink and for heaven's sake try and make merry. What are you thinking about?"

"I was thinking," Escott said, "that to-morrow night some poor devil here may have dropped out of it all. Dropped into some strange place without any money and without friends. And the worst of it all will be that he will know that here it is all going on just the same as it was the night before, when he was

a part of it—the same crowd and the same music—
and that his friends of the night before will laugh
with the rest of them, and that he will be as dead to
them as if he had never lived."

"My!" said Miss Brunelle, "you are a lively com-
panion. Let me count the men here to-night. If they
don't all show up to-morrow, I'm afraid I couldn't
eat my dinner."

And then Miss Brunelle seemed to pull herself together mentally, as it were, and to assume the head
of the table and the rôle of the hostess. She talked
continuously, and laughed over the old days of the
road and her strange experiences as a popular soubrette, the idol of the New England and Pennsylvania circuits. And finally Escott found himself
laughing, too, and asking her many questions, and
her views on people and the events of the day. They
were, perhaps, narrow views, but they were interesting ones because they were somewhat individual and
always amusing. At times it almost seemed to Escott
that the girl was perhaps forcing her fun in her
efforts to keep him interested, but he was hardly
willing to admit that she was capable of making any

serious effort for any cause, and so he credited the flow of spirits to the excellent dinner, which Miss Brunelle seemed to find most grateful. But in time the actress consulted her diamond-studded watch and began to search for her gloves.

Escott called for the check, and when it came he signed it on the back with some deliberation. Then he put the last dollar he owned on the plate and pushed it toward the waiter.

"Don't you ever look at your checks," asked Miss Brunelle, "especially when you sign them?"

"I don't know," he answered. "I can't remember that I ever signed one here before." He turned the bill over and glanced at the amount. It read, "Fourteen dollars and twenty cents."

"Why do you smile?" she asked.

"Oh, I don't know," he answered; "there is something rather comic about that twenty cents. It seems such an unnecessary detail. Do you have to go?"

Escott took Miss Brunelle to the stage-door of the music-hall and then went up into his box. It was warm, and the little theatre looked very bright, and the audience seemed particularly enthusiastic and easily amused. From the stage he looked down on a sea of faces; they all were smiling and seemed so content and fearless of the morrow. Then his glance wandered back to the stage, and he looked curiously at two women who were dancing down to the footlights.

"And," said Escott to himself, "they will be doing that to-morrow night, and the night after, and the night after that. And they will smile as they are smiling now and be quite content."

The performance passed before him as a revolving kaleidoscope, a whirling mass of color and odd lights and fanciful movements. For a moment he tried to steady his thoughts and to hunt out Miss Brunelle. She was standing at the back of the stage and looking, at least so it seemed, directly at him. She smiled and he smiled at her, and then somehow she became blended in the stage-picture again, and was lost in the moving mass of color. He pulled viciously at his cigar and breathed the hot air of the theatre through his nostrils. It was all so very warm and bright, and the music so very tuneful. Yes, it was extremely hard to give it all up. And why should he? No. He would

168

stay on for a day or a week or a month, and drift
with the tide of his own dissipated fortunes. There
must come a turning some day. The curtain was
falling, and he smiled listlessly at the faces of half a
dozen women who were smiling up at him. The
music went on playing the popular song of the burlesque, and he went out humming it to himself.

"Some day," he thought, "I may be humming
that on a prairie or in jail, and it will bring all this
back to me. I must not forget that song. It is so
reminiscent."

At first he decided that he would begin his week
of pleasure at once, and had determined to look up
some of his friends for a little supper-party. And
then the strain of the day began to tell upon him,
and as he walked into the cool air of the streets his
steps seemed to turn instinctively toward home.

When he arrived there he found two notes on his
desk. The first he opened was an invitation to a dinner for the following night.

"Will I go? Rather," he said. "The devil certainly
doesn't seem to lose much time in looking after his
own."

The second note was addressed in pencil, and in an unknown handwriting. He tore off the envelope and found inside the bill for the dinner he had had that night with Miss Brunelle. His glance fell on the familiar fourteen dollars and twenty cents, and then he turned over the soiled slip of paper, and across its back was stamped the name of the restaurant and the word "Paid." Underneath it, in the same handwriting as the envelope, were these lines from Miss Stella Brunelle: "Dear Billy: I told the girls at the theatre that you were going away to-morrow. Going into some sort of business out West (I forget just where). They were very sorry, but they said they would be mighty glad to see you again whenever you got back. Good-by, and God bless you, Billy."

THE CROSS ROADS, NEW YORK

THE CROSS ROADS, NEW YORK

MISS ROSE CAWTHORNE, character woman of the Great Mogul Company, sat with folded hands at the window of her room in the theatrical boarding-house, which for many years she had honored with her patronage. Now and again she glanced through the stiffly starched lace curtains and saw Twenty-second Street deep in new fallen snow, the trees heavy with sparkling icicles, and the air filled with fluttering silver flakes. Inside, a coal fire glowed on the shallow grate and a single burning gas jet gave to the room a certain air of cheerfulness, even though it brought into sharper relief the faded pink carpet and the badly frayed green silk furniture.

As the hands of the nickel alarm clock on the mantel marked the hour of three, Miss Cawthorne unfolded her hands, took the rose-colored knit shawl from her shoulders, once more glanced out through

173

the lace curtains, and then walked to the mirror across the room. For a moment she looked steadily into the glass at the sharply cut features, the faded coloring, the shadows under the eyes, and then with the merest suggestion of a smile glanced down at her well-preserved figure. She opened a "vanity box" that lay on the bureau, and, with the dexterity of one accustomed to making up, lightly touched her lips with rouge and added a little more powder to the already ample supply on her nose and cheeks. Then she patted the curls on her forehead and gently brushed back the bronze-red pompadour. It had been a long time since Miss Cawthorne had anticipated a visit from one of the gilded youth of New York.

It was hardly the room she would have chosen in which to receive her guest; but it was well enough for a theatrical boarding-house, and much more private than the reception-room down stairs. By no reaches of the imagination could the folding bed be taken for any other article of furniture, and the green silk of the chairs was certainly very badly frayed; but there was a table cover of a lively hue, and many

The Cross Roads, New York.

signed photographs of many actresses went far toward covering the faded wall-paper. Once more Miss Cawthorne glanced out at the snow-covered street, and was this time rewarded by the sight of an approaching electric hansom. With an ostentatious clanging of the gong the cab drew up in front of the boarding-house, and the woman returned to her seat at the window.

The colored servant who went to the door had received his instructions, and without delay led the visitor up two flights of stairs to the actress's room. The visitor was a young man, perhaps twenty-five years of age, tall and athletic looking, with a clean, fresh skin and fine clear eyes that spoke of health and a total lack of care and worry. Miss Cawthorne unfolded her hands and rose from her chair with more sprightliness than she had originally planned. "It was very good of you to come, Mr. Brandt," she said, extending her hand. "I have seen you sitting on the front row at our performance so often now that I really look upon you as an old friend."

"It was very good of you to ask me," said young Brandt, bending over until his lips almost touched the diamonds on the powdered hand. She held him away from her at arm's length, and under the hanging gas jet looked steadily into the young man's clear blue eyes.

"You are very like your father," she said, "in your looks, and more especially in your manner."

"Oh, then you knew my father?"

"Yes, a long time ago. You must accept that as my apology for asking you here. Your father had a certain courtesy, even courtliness in his manner, that was quite old fashioned, but I am sure all women loved him for it. I think there must be much of the same charm in the son; that is, if I am to believe all the things I hear of him. Won't you sit down?"

Miss Cawthorne returned to her arm chair at the window; but Brandt walked over to the hearth, and stood warming his hands behind his back, and smiling at his hostess.

"I suppose you refer to my friends in the Mogul Company?" he said. "I really hope they do like me. You've all given me such a lot of fun. I don't know what I should do if the Mogul left town."

Miss Cawthorne looked up and smiled at him, the

meantime beating a tattoo on the padded arms of her chair. "Oh, they like you very much; they're forever talking of your parties, and they show me the flowers and things you send them. Especially little Miss Page; she and I are great pals—such a nice girl! She told me yesterday all about the wonderful supper you are having for her to-night. It must be very pleasant to be able to give all that happiness. Very different from the old days at Selbyville, I imagine."

The young man nodded. "Yes, very different," he said. "It was certainly quiet enough there. My father, you know, was always devoted to his flowers and his books, and until the last his writing was his greatest amusement. Neither he nor my mother cared very much about going around with other people. So you can understand Selbyville was not very gay for me, and when my mother died there seemed to be no particular reason for my staying on."

"And so," said Miss Cawthorne, smiling, and with a certain ornate manner of the stage, "you left the old home, and, bringing your fortune with you, came to the great city, and there you discovered content on the front row of the Casino theatre, and complete happiness in the girlish smiles of little Maizie Page."

Brandt nodded his head slowly. "I must confess that it is the best chair I have found so far in New York, and Miss Page's smiles are quite wonderful. Don't you think so?"

Miss Cawthorne looked out of the window until the glare of the glistening snow made her turn her eyes back to the soft light of the room and to the fresh, pleasant face of the young man standing in front of the fireplace. "I suppose they are quite wonderful," she said slowly; "but then, you see, I am a fairly old woman now, and have seen a great many wonderful smiles from the stage to the front row, and they all meant such very different things from what they were supposed to mean. Sometimes they were meant to show a row of good teeth or a pair of dimples; and sometimes they were meant to appease the stage manager in the prompt entrance, or make the musical director or their particular friend in the orchestra jealous; or very often they were meant to make the rest of the audience think that the owner of the smile had at least one admirer on the front row or in the boxes. It is wonderful how really insincere most stage smiles are. But of course Miss Page's smile may be different. They tell me you are really very devoted; they have even suggested that you thought of marriage."

The color slowly crept into the young man's face, and he half raised his hand in protest.

Miss Cawthorne quickly rose from her chair. "Don't—please don't!" she begged. "I'm so sorry! I didn't mean to say that."

Brandt went over to the table and picked up his gloves and hat. "Really, Miss Cawthorne, I don't want to be uncivil," he said, "nor unappreciative; but I can't understand why you should take such an interest in Miss Page and me."

Miss Cawthorne walked toward the door, as if in an attempt to prevent Brandt leaving the room, and then turned and held out her hand toward him. "I'm very sorry," she said—"it was so clumsy of me! I know that I'm only a stranger. Please forgive me—please! It wasn't what I wanted to say at all."

Brandt nodded gravely. "May I ask you then what you did want to say?"

"Why yes," she said. "It was really nothing—just an incident that I thought might interest you. Please sit down, won't you, or go back there and stand by the fire? I don't want to think you are going away at once. I wanted so much to be good friends with you."

Brandt put down his hat and gloves and went back to his old place in front of the grate. The actress sat at a little marble centre-table, leaning her elbows on it and resting her chin between the palms of her hands.

"It's not a very pleasant story for me to tell," she said, looking up at Brandt, "but it won't take long. It's about your mother."

The young man looked at her with much curiosity, even a certain incredulity; so far as he knew, his mother had never known any one who was in any way connected with the stage.

"Do you see that large panel photograph over there on the piano?" Miss Cawthorne said, without changing her position. "I mean the very old faded one, of the girl in the black tights, and the close fitting basque, and the foolish hat with the plumes?

180

Well, that's I—twenty-five years ago—or more, perhaps. Just think, that was taken before you were born!"

Brandt picked up the photograph and carried it to the light. "It is very, very beautiful indeed," he said.

"That was my first great success. We played the piece here in New York for nearly a year; and that was a wonderful year for me. I was just about twenty then, and the days never seemed quite long enough for all the pleasures I tried to squeeze into them. You see, I was young, and had health to spare, and was almost famous in a small way. Then men about town and the boys from college used to fill the front rows every night, and there were always suppers and flowers and big dinners on Sunday nights. I was as well known then as—well, as Maizie Page is to-day."

Miss Cawthorne stopped and smiled up at Brandt. There was a new light in the gray eyes he had never seen before, and the blood had risen to her temples and darkened the faded cheeks. Brandt saw for the first time the likeness between the girl of the faded photograph and the present character woman of the Mogul Company.

"Please go on," he said.

"We stayed in New York almost a year, and near the end of the season a manager named Hanson— he was a friend of mine whom I liked very much at the time—offered to make a star of me. You know how that appeals to every actress. The difficulty was to get a play that would suit me. I had some fine ideas then, and refused to go into musical comedy, which was the only thing I really could do. I insisted it was to be straight drama. So at last we got hold of a comedy through a play agent. It was called 'In the Best Regulated Families,' and I think it was the first and the last play your father ever wrote. We liked it for two reasons—it had one good scene, and it was cheap. We knew that Mr. Brandt was rich and wrote only for pleasure, so we got it for almost nothing. We opened in Troy, and for a comedy it turned out one of the most dire tragedies I have ever known. The play was not so bad, but the company was awful, and I was so nervous I didn't know whether I was up stage or at home eating supper.

"When the performance was over I went back to the hotel, and I think I really wanted to die The manager, Hanson, came up to my room and told me just how bad I had been, and he was pretty rough about it, too. You see, he had lost everything he owned, and he was sore. Besides that, he was a brute. He swore at me for a while, and then—then—well, he struck me."

The actress stopped talking, and rubbed her hand slowly across her eyes, as if to shut out the memory of that night twenty-five years before. Then she glanced up at the young man standing at the fireplace, looking down at her with grave, sympathetic eyes.

"He struck me here," the actress began again, pointing to her shoulder near the throat, "and then he left me alone and went down stairs to talk to your father about the play. He left me alone lying on the bed, hurt and bruised, and my heart was breaking. And there I lay sobbing aloud and crying for the old days back on Broadway and the good friends I had had then—the college boys and the suppers and everything I loved. You see I was really only a girl at the time, and I hadn't quite got used to the knocks and bumps that came later.

"I don't know how long I lay there crying, but after a time I heard the door open, and your mother came in. She was very young and very pretty. I had never met her, but she had been pointed out to me as your father's wife—she was just a bride, then. She had the next room to mine, and I suppose she must have heard Hanson swearing and then my sobs. She sat on the edge of the bed and tried to comfort me about the play, and you can imagine it was pretty hard for her, because she knew nothing about plays, or actors either, I guess. And all the time she kept her hand on the bruised place on my shoulder where Hanson had struck me, just to pretend that she didn't notice it. Anyhow, I went to sleep in her arms, and when I woke the next morning she and your father had gone back to Selbyville. They sent me some flowers afterward, and I wrote a letter to her; but I never saw them again."

Miss Cawthorne walked over to the window, and, parting the lace curtains, stood for some moments looking out on the scurrying snowflakes. Then she turned back to her guest.

"And so, you see," she said, "when I heard them

gossiping about you at the theatre, and I learned who you were, I wanted to meet you, because you were the son of your mother, and of your father."

"And you don't know how I appreciate it," said Brandt. "I'm awfully sorry I spoke as I did a little while ago while you were talking of my friendship for Miss Page. But, really, she seems such an unusually nice girl to me. I don't know when I have met any one who was sweeter or better bred in every way."

Miss Cawthorne nodded. "You're quite right— she is very nice, and very, very good to her people. Do you know her mother?"

"I did meet her once, but it was just for a moment at the stage door. It was so dark I don't suppose I should know her again if I saw her."

While Brandt was talking, Miss Cawthorne leaned against the window sash, looking down on the snow-covered streets, deserted save for the black cab at the door.

"Look, Mr. Brandt!" she said suddenly. "It is clearing at last, and the sun is really coming out. Isn't it beautiful? I don't suppose that you would care to take me up to Miss Page's now, would you?

185

You see, I promised to loan her something for the supper to-night, and I'm sure she would rather have it before she goes to the theatre."

"I'd be only too glad," Brandt said with enthusiasm. "The electric can get us there in no time."

As they turned into West Forty-ninth Street Brandt began to recognize the houses he had seen before only at night when he had driven Miss Page home after supper. "Now I begin to feel at home," he said. "It's funny I have never been here in the daylight, isn't it?"

"Yes," replied Miss Cawthorne, "in a way it is."

The cab stopped in front of a high brick apartment house, and Miss Cawthorne and Brandt went up into a narrow vestibule and looked for Miss Page's name under one of the many brass letter boxes. They found it at last, and in response to their ring the catch of the front door clicked violently, and they pushed on into a dark, narrow hallway. Miss Cawthorne had been there before, so she led the way to the winding stairway in the rear. The air was stuffy and damp, and at the first step Brandt caught his foot in a hole in the dirty, badly patched carpet. Slowly they climbed five flights of twisting stairs. At the landings, slatternly looking women and children with dirty faces and bare legs came out to stare at them in open-mouthed wonder; a man in his shirt sleeves and without a collar stood at the door of his apartment and looked them over with insolent curiosity, and a dog at his heels barked and snapped at the actress's dress. At the fifth landing they found Miss Page's mother waiting in semidarkness for her unknown guests. A beautiful Pomeranian dog, which Brandt had once owned, dashed out of the doorway and leaped up, in an effort to kiss the hand of its former master. At the moment, the little thoroughbred, with its lithe, trim legs and beautiful soft coat, seemed to Brandt to be curiously out of place.

Mrs. Page led them through the narrow hallway to the sitting-room, which was at the far end of the flat, and then disappeared. A very stout old man sat in a rocking chair by the window and read the evening paper. He was in his shirt sleeves, and smoked a heavy pipe, and rocked continuously. Just beyond this room there was another smaller one, where they found Maizie Page. She had been dozing on a lounge, which had been arranged as a cozy corner, and she received them sleepily and with evident surprise. The walls of the room were for the most part covered with a net, in the meshes of which had been arranged many photographs of actresses and actors and of a few who were not of the stage. There were many flags and long streamers of nearly all the colleges, and tin horns and great wooden rattles, decorated with varicolored ribbons, and cheap fans and souvenir dolls from the restaurants. From a window opening on a broad court the afternoon sun fell in a broad, unbroken shaft of soft orange light. Surrounded by this riot of color, Miss Page, dressed in a pink kimono, continued for some moments to gaze with undisguised wonderment at her guests.

"But how was it you came together?" she said at last. "I didn't know you knew Arthur."

"I didn't until this afternoon," Miss Cawthorne explained a little hurriedly. "He came to see me about another matter, and it occurred to me you might want to fix these buckles before you started for the theatre, so I asked him to bring me up in his cab."

Miss Page was wide awake now, and as Miss Cawthorne faltered through her speech, the young girl looked directly into the older woman's eyes. "It was good of you," she said. "You have the buckles with you?"

Miss Cawthorne fumbled nervously with the clasp of the reticule that she held in her hand, while Miss Page stood waiting quietly, her thin, colorless lips pressed into a straight line. At last the package containing the buckles was found, and Miss Cawthorne nervously gave it into Miss Page's hand. The girl walked over to a closet, and, opening the door, placed the package on a high shelf, which was littered with many soiled silk slippers and a discarded sailor hat. Against the wall of the shallow closet and on some hooks on the inside of the door were several filmy dresses and silk petticoats. In the daylight the clothes seemed to look particularly unfresh, and the tiny spangles and the embroidery very cheap and tawdry. Miss Page looked over her shoulder at her guests, and then pushed the door wide open.

"There!" she said. "Do you see them, Arthur?

Those are the Cinderella clothes that I wear after dark."

From one of the hooks the girl pulled a white batiste skirt and waist and flung them out in front of her, so that they fell directly in the shaft of yellow sunshine. The skirt was badly crumpled, and the seam-binding of the waist was far from fresh.

"That," she said, "is the dress I am going to wear to your party this evening. It doesn't look very well now, but it'll be fine to-night under the gaslight, I promise you." The girl walked to the doorway. "Mother!" she called. "Mother, I want you to come in here for a moment."

Mrs. Page's voice came indistinctly from a room down the hallway. "I can't just now, dear."

"Yes," called the girl—"I want you to come at once; just as you are, please."

The mother came slowly down the hallway and hesitated at the door, until her daughter took her hand and led her into the sunlight. Her black hair, streaked with gray, hung loosely about her bent shoulders, the sleeves of her striped flannel wrapper were rolled up above the elbows, and on her feet she wore an old pair of woollen slippers. With one hand she held the gaping, soiled wrapper together, and with the other brushed loose strands of hair from her eyes.

"You must pardon me, Mr. Brandt," she said. "I've been in the kitchen getting the supper ready— my old man gets hungry pretty early."

"I'm very glad indeed to meet you," Brandt said.

Mrs. Page wiped her hand on her apron, made a half bow, half courtesy, and shook her guest warmly by the hand. Then she glanced at her daughter and got a nod of permission to leave them. Miss Page glanced into the next room where the old man was smoking.

"I'm afraid I'd better not introduce you to my father—he's very busy reading."

And then the girl and her two guests, standing in the centre of the room, looked one to the other and for some moments remained silent. The visit and its object, if object there had been, were accomplished, and there seemed no reason now for staying on. It was Miss Cawthorne who spoke first.

"It's been so nice to see you, Maizie. We must be

going now—that is, if Mr. Brandt will take me home again."

Brandt nodded.

"I'll see you to-night, dear," Miss Cawthorne called back from the hallway.

For the moment Maizie Page and Brandt were alone.

"Good-by," he said, shaking hands with her. "It's been very good to have seen you in your own home."

The girl, still holding his hand, looked up and tried to smile through dimmed eyes. "I'm glad you liked my home," she said simply. "I didn't think you would. That's why I didn't ask you here before." The girl half turned and looked about the little room, gaudy with its cheap decorations—at the faded photographs, the college flags, and the paper dolls, and then she glanced beyond to the old man in his shirt sleeves, smoking his pipe in the next room.

"Hurry up, Mr. Brandt!" Miss Cawthorne called from the end of the hallway.

"Good-by," said Maizie Page. "I'll see you to-night after the performance?"

192

"Of course," he said, and raising her hand to his lips, kissed the tips of her fingers.

Miss Cawthorne and Brandt settled back in the cushions of the cab, and were far on their way down town before either of them spoke.

"Did you enjoy your visit?" the actress said at last.

Brandt shrugged his shoulders. "Did you expect me to enjoy it?" he asked. "Did you mean it as a kindness to me?"

Miss Cawthorne looked straight ahead through the window in the front of the hansom. "I did it for you and for the girl—I knew you didn't understand the type—I wanted you to start fair with her. Thanks to men like yourself, she knows two kinds of life—you know only one."

"How did you know I didn't know about her home?"

"I guessed it—I've known a good many of that type—show business in New York is full of them."

"What is the type?" he asked.

"It's the type that the outside public can't believe exists—I mean the girl who is morally good, and

193

yet who accepts every kind of present from a man except money, eats caviare at lunch and terrapin at supper, and is lucky if she has bacon with her coffee in the morning. They walk to the theatre at night and drive home after supper in an electric cab, and they live west of Eighth Avenue to save five dollars in the month's rent."

"And what is the finish of that kind of life?" he asked.

"The finish is that they usually marry the man who plays the cymbals in the orchestra, or the chief usher, or the assistant treasurer in the box office, or a cousin of their mother's who is a widower with three children and lives in Brooklyn."

"And then?" asked Brandt.

"After they are married their husbands pawn the jewels and everything else their admirers gave them, except the photographs of the admirers themselves— which might seem careless, but isn't. That is because the women don't care at all about the admirers who used to give them violets, but are quite crazy about their husbands who now give them black eyes."

They were nearly home, and for a moment the

cab was blocked at the corner where Fifth Avenue and Broadway cross at Twenty-third Street.

"New York is a wonderful city, just at this corner, isn't it?" the actress ran on—"just at this hour especially, with all the crowds and the carriages and the automobiles. It's fine! Did you ever hear of Billy Straight?"

Brandt shook his head.

"Of course not—he was before your day. Billy was a great friend of mine. He called this corner 'The Crossroads,' and he used to tell a funny story about his father stopping here late one evening, just after he had come home to live after leaving college, and showing him the two streets—Fifth Avenue all dark and gloomy—there were brownstone dwellings then right down to Twenty-sixth Street—and then he pointed up Broadway, all ablaze with lights, and the doors wide open. 'You can take your choice, my boy,' the old man said—'both roads are open to you. It's the question every kid with money and a position has got to decide for himself in New York—and every other town, I guess, too, only the game is bigger here and harder to fight.'"

195

The cab had started again, and they were nearing Miss Cawthorne's home.

"Well," said the young man, "what road did Billy take?"

The actress smiled. "He started up the avenue all right enough; but he turned off to Broadway one night, and he never got back again. They never do."

The cab came to a sudden stop at Miss Cawthorne's door. "Poor old Billy!" said the woman.

Brandt helped her out of the hansom. "Good-by, Miss Cawthorne. It was very kind of you to ask me to come to see you. Thank you for the visit and the story about The Crossroads, too."

The actress smiled, and held out her hand. "You mustn't mention that," she said. "I didn't expect or want you to thank me; I somehow felt that I owed it to your mother. We didn't have much in common and we led very different kinds of lives, but I guess all old women feel pretty much the same way about some things. I'm almost sure that she would have thanked me—Good-night."

THE KIDNAPPERS

THE KIDNAPPERS

IT was about seven o'clock in the evening when I returned to my apartment and found the telegram: It read:

Meet me if possible at Begum to-night, ten-thirty. Important.

WALTER WAINRIGHT.

My friend Wainwright might have been a great financier, or a famous author, or an ambassador to a European court, or he might have been pretty much anything else that required an extremely quick and creative intelligence; but he was, and is, a theatrical manager.

When I first entered the theatre that night in response to his telegram, I found the second act of "The Begum of Bo" well under way, and Wainwright leaning on the railing at the rear of the orchestra seats. With a pained expression he was gazing at

199

the stage. "Comedians like those," he said, "should be arrested for grand larceny. They steal their stuff from real actors, and then rob the public. Eh?"

I nodded. "What did you want?" I asked.

Wainwright pressed his lips into a straight line and blinked his eyes as if his brain was confused with many thoughts. "I'm very busy," he said; "but I think you can help me a good deal. Have you anything to do for the next half hour?"

"Nothing," I said, "for several half hours."

"That's good—that's good," he mumbled, his mind still apparently active with many thoughts. "If you will go back now on the stage and look on the prompt side, just in front of the switchboard, you will see a beautiful lady in street costume. You may think it's a tent, with flowers trailing over it; but it's not—that's her hat—and under it you will see a really beautiful lady. Tell her I said that she was to follow you, and you will probably find her fairly docile. Lead her out of the stage door, and there you will see a closed hack with a couple of dress-suit cases and a driver in front. Tell the driver to take you to the Forty-second Street station, and when you arrive pay the cabby his fare and lead the girl to gate number twelve. Say 'Company' to the ticket man, and the girl will do the rest."

"And where do you come in?" I asked.

"I come in before the train starts—don't worry."

"All right," I said, and started for the little door that leads from the auditorium to the stage. There certainly was a girl standing in front of the switchboard on the prompt side, and she wore a spreading hat with a great many flowers on it. It was with some little difficulty that I pushed my way through a small army of short-skirted flower-girls and armored warriors with very prickly tin spears, who were waiting to go on the stage. At last I reached the side of the lady and bowed in my most respectful manner.

"Pardon me, madam," I apologized, "but Mr. Wainwright says that you are to come with me."

The girl looked up at me, I thought a little wistfully, and without more ado took my arm.

Slowly we picked our way through the mob of flower-girls and warriors, and at last reached the door leading to the street. There stood the cab with the suit cases in front: so I put the lady in and told the driver to take us with all speed to the Grand Central station. It is seldom I meet a lady of whom I know absolutely nothing—I had even forgotten to ask Wainwright her name. For the first time, I believe, in my life I found conversation most difficult; so I casually remarked, "It's a very bad night for such a beautiful hat."

At this the girl turned deliberately from me and stared out of the window, which struck me as peculiarly uncomplimentary, as she could see nothing but the deserted, storm-swept streets. Fortunately, we had not very far to go, and my only other remark was, I believe, "Ah, here we are!"

I helped the lady to alight, paid the cabman, and, seizing a suit case in either hand, led her through the station to gate Number Twelve.

"Company," said I to the guard at the gate, and passed on.

At this point a middle-aged individual, having rather the appearance of a plain-clothes man from police head-quarters, respectfully bowed to the lady, and relieved me of the dress-suit cases. Preceding

us to a sleeping car, he opened the door of a compartment, and, putting down the suit cases, delivered
himself of a profound salaam and bowed himself
away. No sooner had he left us than the spirits of
the lady seemed at once to revive. She took off the
large hat and showed a wonderful mass of golden
brown hair, which was worn high over her broad
clear forehead.

"Come in," she said, turning to me as I stood
hesitating in the doorway.

For some moments we sat in the compartment in
silence, regarding each other with much apparent
curiosity and amusement.

"Why have I never seen you before?" I asked at
last, and it really seemed to me then as if I should
have known her always. At the moment I could not
understand how a girl with such beauty and a personality that could take possession of me as hers had
done should not be known to every one.

"You have seen me before on the stage," she said,
"I have often seen you."

"It doesn't seem quite possible." I protested.

"On the contrary, almost every one in the com-

pany at least knew who you were. I was quite unknown to fame then, and am now, and shall be until
Wednesday."

"What!" I said; but I said no more, for I felt the
car give a sudden jolt and then move evenly forward
on its way out of the station. I jumped to my feet
and turned to the door; but while I had been talking
to my beautiful friend some one had closed it, and
when I tried the knob I found that it had been
locked as well. I turned back to the girl and found
her looking at me with crinkled brow and the tips of
her mouth pointed upward in an amused smile. I regained my composure as well as I could and started
toward the electric button.

"Apparently we are locked in," I said cheerfully.

"Apparently," she replied. "It's not worth while
ringing the bell—no one will come."

I sat down and smiled back at her smiling eyes.
"Am I kidnapped?" I asked.

At that moment there was a knock at the door.
"There is Wainwright," she said; "I think I'll let
him explain."

The door opened, and Wainwright came in. He

was actually grinning at me, and apparently perfectly delighted with himself.

"Well," I asked, "is this your idea of a joke?"

He sat down at the end of the long lounge opposite me and tapped the end of his boot with the ferule of his cane.

"Not a joke at all," he said briskly—"business, theatrical business. Now listen sharply, please, because I have to get off at One Hundred and Twenty-fifth Street, and of course, if you wish to get off with me I can't prevent you. Have you met Miss Abercrombie?"

I bowed in the direction of the lady. "I have had the honor of chatting with her for some few moments."

Wainwright stopped grinning and suddenly became serious—that is, as serious as he ever could be. "Miss Abercrombie—Alice Abercrombie—is a find of mine; I discovered her playing a small part in one of my own comic-opera companies and was attracted by her beauty, and then by her unusual intelligence. I decided then that I would make her the greatest woman star in America. For two years I have made her work in road companies, and have spent large

205

sums in having her taught how to sing and dance;
all of the other accomplishments she already had.
Now I think she is ready to star. I have booked her
in 'The Princess Popinjay,' beginning next Wednesday, for ten days of one-night stands before she
opens at Denver. I intend to have her make a sensation out there, and come to New York this spring
with the rumor of a Western furore back of her. She
is going to do in comic opera what Mary Anderson
did in Shakespeare thirty years ago, or I shall miss
my guess and lose a great deal of money."

"And where do I come in?" I asked.

"You must help create the furore. At some time in
the career of every great male star, and it usually
happened when his business was very bad, he has
been pursued by a beautiful veiled lady, and the
same thing applies to every woman star, only the
mysterious stranger was a man. Now you are to be
the mysterious stranger, only with a few new varia-
tions. I chose you for the part because you have a
particularly showy wardrobe and a sense of humor.
I have had the press agent ahead of the show feature
you about as prominently as Miss Abercrombie. In

some towns you will find yourself referred to as a well-known American iron king, sometimes as an Austrian count, and again as a titled Englishman. If you read the local papers in the towns you visit, you will find your picture prominently displayed."

"My picture!" I gasped. "I haven't had my photograph taken for twenty years!"

"Please don't interrupt," said Wainwright— "we're out of the tunnel already. The photographs are some I found in my office—mostly of bad actors looking for a job."

"And this wardrobe you are pleased to speak of so flatteringly?" I demanded.

"I telephoned your man about that while you were out dining this evening. It is all in the state room in the next car. By referring to the morning papers in each town, you can find out whether you are an Austrian count, titled Englishman, or plain American iron magnate and then you can register as such and dress accordingly. You will, of course, be interviewed by the local papers, and must express yourself freely. Do you know anything about Austria?"

"Nothing," I said.

"Well, the main street of Vienna is called 'The Ringstrasse,' and the parliament is generally known as the Reichsrath. You will also probably be asked about the politics at home. Of course you know all about England. I forget just what county your family came from over there; but here you are naturally a Pittsburger, where you live with your folks, who hate your devotion to Miss Abercrombie, the beautiful actress."

"Pardon me," I said; "but why could you not have explained all this to me at supper last night?"

"Perfectly simple," he replied suavely. "Because, surrounded as you were then by all the flesh-pots of town, you would have refused. Under existing conditions, how can you?" and he bowed low to Miss Abercrombie.

"Pardon me again," I asked; "but am I supposed to know the lady?"

"Certainly," said Wainwright a little peevishly at my stupidity. "You must be seen dining with her occasionally, and always with sad, hungry eyes. You see, she doesn't really like you: she is wedded to her art. At night you must sit in an upper stage box and——"

"Look sad and hungry?" I suggested.

"That's it—sad and hungry."

"How about my engagements in town for the next two weeks?"

"That's all right. Wire your servant to advise your friends that you've been called away on important business. Understand, don't you wire direct, or some one might know where you are. I want you to lose yourself entirely. And above all be a sport—don't lose your sense of humor entirely. Think of being the only man in New York I thought worth kidnapping! You are always complaining about the dulness of the long days and the adventureless nights. Now you've got all the adventure you'll want."

The train gradually began to slow down. Wainwright jumped up and opened the door of the compartment. "Here's Harlem, and I must leave you. And, I say, don't forget to look me up when you get back. I really want to hear what you think of the play. Good-by, children."

I, too, jumped to my feet. "Why don't you go

yourself?" I shouted at him somewhat ungallantly just as the train came to a full stop.

"No!" he said. "I couldn't stand that route, not even with Alice along." He waved his cane at us, the door slammed in my face, and I heard him chuckling loudly as he hurried by the compartment on his way to the platform. I turned and looked at the raised eyebrows and big searching eyes of the actress looking into my own.

"And you didn't want to go," she said very slowly; "really, did you?"

Our train was moving again so I sat down on the edge of the green velvet lounge and looked beyond her out of the blurred window pane at the glistening station platform and the slowly passing houses with their dripping roofs. Through my mind there flashed the thought of many pleasant things I had promised myself for the next two weeks. Then I turned back to the girl and found her looking at me as I knew she would look, just as I know the photograph of her on the mantel back of me is looking at me now.

"Of course I wanted to come," I said; "but really that doesn't make much difference, because when you open your eyes wide and crinkle your brow, I would follow you, I think, to almost any place. I'm willing to admit that I'm kidnapped; but by a beautiful woman, not by any fool trick of Wainwright."

The girl shrugged her shoulders, smiled, and leaned back against the cushions in the corner of the compartment.

"Good-night," I said, as I rose from the lounge.

She nodded to me and, still smiling, folded her arms.

I found the manager in the next car, and he greeted me with the same servile grin with which he had met us at the train gate.

"I'm Ben Adler," he said. "I'm travelling with the show, and my instructions are to make you as comfortable as possible."

"It seems to me," I answered somewhat crisply, "that if you follow your instructions, you ought to make me pretty uncomfortable, with your Austrian counts and titled Englishmen and your interviews. Where do I sleep, anyhow? Is this a special train?"

Adler grinned. "Of course it's a special train— we're travelling in great style. Your compartment is at the end of this car; but there's a cold lunch up ahead. Perhaps you would like to meet some of the company?"

I was nervous and far from sleepy; so I followed him to the forward car, which was a day coach. It was filled with perhaps thirty women and about half as many men. In the aisle there was a long case partly filled with bottles of stout and beer, and on one of the seats there was a tray of thick sandwiches. Nearly all of the men were smoking cigars or pipes, and a few of the women cigarettes. The car was stuffy and hot and the smoke so thick that it was difficult at first to recognize the faces about me. A show girl whom I once had met at supper greeted me cordially.

"It's funny to see you here," she said. "I didn't know Wainwright was with the show."

"He's not," Adler interrupted; "the gentleman's a friend of Miss Abercrombie. He's going with us as far as Denver."

"My word!" said the show girl. "Shake hands with my chum, Miss Armstrong. Rita, wake up— you're not in Philadelphia!"

THE KIDNAPPERS

Miss Armstrong was a large, heavy-eyed girl dressed in a shirtwaist and she wore a great deal of cheap jewelry. "Pleased to meet you," she mumbled, pulling herself out of the hot plush seat. "What name, please?"

"Come on," interrupted Adler. "I want you to meet some of the principals."

"Just fancy!" said Miss Armstrong. "Really, you know, we can't all be principals." Then she yawned and snuggled back into the corner to resume her interrupted doze.

As we walked down the aisle, the girls lying back in the seats eyed us with a certain bovine interest, and those who were sufficiently awake and not too engrossed with the sandwiches commented audibly on the honor of my unexpected presence. At the far end of the car we found a party of four—two men and two women playing hearts. There was Baker, who I learned afterward was the second comedian, and who imagined that he ought to be continually comic off as well as on the stage; Carroll, who in the opera played the lover lieutenant in the inevitable white duck uniform, and who was a third-class Englishman; Miss Belden, the rough soubrette of the company; and a very young and pretty girl named Ryan, who played a small part, and who, it seemed to me, rather outclassed her present company. They stopped playing cards long enough to shake hands with me and express their pleasure that I was to be of the party for so long a time. Miss Belden crowded over toward Carroll and gave me a nodded invitation to sit on the arm of the chair next to her.

"Make my friend comfortable," said Adler, and he left us. The card players resumed their game. A small, black-eyed chorus girl moved over from her place across the aisle and sat on the arm of the seat opposite me and next to Baker. "Have some?" she said, holding out a tumbler half filled with beer; but I thanked her and declined.

"Back, back, little one!" Baker growled. "Take your arm off the back of my seat, and don't butt in!"

"What are you playing?" said the girl without moving.

"Hearts at a dollar a point."

"My!" said the chorus girl. "Ain't it wonderful how you Broadway comedians can gamble on forty

214

a week! Did you hear the name of that town we open at? It's a flag station on a trolley line, I think."

"Prescott's a good town," said Miss Ryan. "Miss Abercrombie has played there before."

"Is it possible?" said the chorus girl. "I suppose they'll meet her with a brass band, and the town constable will make a speech and give her a dollar watch from the stage. It's great to be an established star."

"She's a friend of this gentleman here," said Miss Belden, sorting her cards.

The chorus girl looked at me with apparently renewed interest and smiled her apology. "I guess I'm out of my set. Me for bed. Good-night, all!"

The car had become very quiet now, as all the women had either curled up on the plush seats or gone to their berths in the other cars. The card players gambled on in silence, and as it seemed this might continue indefinitely, I, too, bade them good-night and went to my compartment.

When the porter called me the next day he announced that they had put on a restaurant car; and so when I was dressed I went out and ordered my breakfast. It was too early for the members of the company to be about, and I found myself quite alone. We had already travelled far from home, and were racing through what was, at least to me, a very new and beautiful country. The car itself was fresh, and the air was clean and a most pleasant contrast to the day coach of the night before. Outside it was a wonderful cloudless morning in early January, and under the blue sky the trees, dripping with icicles, shimmered and sparkled in the morning sun, and the land stretched out as one great field of unbroken snow.

Before my breakfast had been served Alice Abercrombie came in and sat down on the other side of my little table. She was dressed in a simple shirtwaist and a short cloth skirt, and her eyes were as bright and her skin as clear and fresh as the winter day itself.

"Good-morning. And what do you think of trouping?" she said, reaching out her hand to me across the table.

"To be candid," I replied, "it apparently varies more or less. I had the pleasure of meeting the company after I left you last night, and the car they were in seems to have left rather unpleasant recollections of flat beer and stale smoke. But this is fine, isn't it? What are you going to have for breakfast?"

Miss Abercrombie looked out of the window at the stretches of glistening snow, and the smile vanished. "I haven't met many of the chorus," she said. "I thought they seemed a rather good sort at rehearsal."

"I didn't refer to the company," I interrupted— "I only said that the car was stuffy. As a matter of fact, they seemed rather too engrossed in their game of cards last night for me to interrupt. I thought Miss Ryan very pretty to look at."

Miss Abercrombie raised her eyebrows. "I suppose she is pretty."

"Did you ever travel like that?" I asked, nodding to the forward car.

"You ask such simple, direct questions," she said. "If you mean did I ever travel in day coaches with the company, I certainly did. Personally, I am not partial to cards, and I prefer clear air to tobacco smoke; but one can read a good book, even a helpful book, and at the same time breathe bad air. I never had any choice—this is the first time I ever had a compartment in a sleeping car."

"You weren't always in this business?" I said.

The girl shook her head. "You're so naïf that I really can't help answering you. No, my life had nothing to do with the stage until the last few years; but a few years is long enough to make one appreciate the drawing-room on a Pullman. It has all the privacy of the hall bedroom in my boarding-house on Forty-eighth Street, and the furnishing is wonderfully better."

"But you prefer the hall bedroom and—and Broadway?"

The girl looked up sharply, and her big eyes flashed at me. "I didn't say anything about Broadway—there are many other streets in New York, although most men think because a woman is on the stage that she doesn't know it."

"I am sorry," I said, and I meant it.

Miss Abercrombie shrugged her shoulders. "There are other streets," she said, "and there are other restaurants than Martin's and Rector's, and there are other places to take afternoon tea than the Waldorf and the Plaza. For instance, there is the hall bedroom I was talking about on Forty-eighth Street,

218

away over on the West Side, where you can get a cup of tea. The kettle is made of tin and badly dented, and the cups are chipped and the oil lamp smokes; but it doesn't smell of musk, and one is not wedged in by a hundred befurred and bevioleted ladies from the upper West Side. You probably wouldn't care for the room, because it's different—different from what you know and different from what you would expect. The carpet is ragged and full of holes; but I love every hole in it. There is also a rip in the seat of the rocking-chair, and everything sags, even the bed; but I have slept there so long that every bump and every billow of it I regard as an old friend."

"It must be a wonderful room," I said, "to have you care for it as you do. What else is there?"

The girl pushed her plate away from her and talked on. "Well, as a matter of fact, there isn't much else. There are some photographs which I take away on the road, and a shelf of books that a few men sent me who know that there are shops in New York where you can buy something else besides American beauties and a bunch of violets with purple tassels."

"And now that you are a star," I asked, "you will go back to Forty-eighth Street?"

The girl rested the tips of her fingers of both hands before her on the edge of the table and drew back in her chair. She looked at me with wide-open eyes, as if my question had suggested all the changes that were to come with her new life.

"No," she said, "I can't go back there. I'll have to go to an apartment hotel, and eat in a dining-room with palms and mirrors—won't I?—and have my meals at regular hours, and build up my health that the quick lunches and the all-night restaurants broke down long ago."

"As bad as that?" I asked.

"You don't know what the road life is—I mean to live it, year in and year out. It isn't the acting; but it's the everlasting travel and the dressing in dirty damp rooms and the eating when you get the chance —sometimes starving just because there is no place to eat. And then, when our digestion is gone, and the very life has been sapped out of us, somebody writes us a song or a wonderful part, and we make a hit, and they turn the spotlight on us, and give us a drawing-room in a sleeping car, and a maid, and a cab to the hotel."

"But there are the helpful books that you admit can be read in smoking cars, and there is always the prospect of New York and the friends waiting for you there."

The girl stared at me and shook her head. "But the friends don't always wait. They forget us in time, because they find new friends; and then we wish we were back on the road again with our own—our own, do you understand; not the chance acquaintance, but the women and men we work and live and play with."

"Your own?" I repeated.

"Yes, my own. There are no outsiders in this business. You must be in it, and of it, or you can't exist in it. It's a life all of itself, and down in our hearts we love it."

"Notwithstanding," I said, "I never met any one on the stage just like you. You're—well, you're different."

The girl looked at me evenly in the eyes and smiled. "Every one is different. Did you ever know any woman in any walk of life who was like any other woman? I may dress differently from some of those girls you saw last night, and may live differently, and may read books instead of the evening papers; but we all belong just as much——"

"Just as much," I interrupted, "as I don't belong."

"Just as much," she repeated, "as you don't and can't belong." Miss Abercrombie smiled and rose from the table. "Here are some of your friends of last night. Come and see me later on in the drawing-room."

She stepped aside to let Baker, the second comedian, go by, and as she did so he patted her familiarly on the shoulder and gave her arm a gentle squeeze.

"Good-morning, little girl," he said genially.

She followed him with her eyes down the aisle and then turned to me, crinkled her brow, and smiled. "You see," she said, "we are one people. Come back and see me soon, Mr. Outsider. Don't forget you are here as my professional admirer, not as Miss Ryan's, or some of those wonderful show girls."

Later I went back to visit Miss Abercrombie; and there it was that I spent most of that day and the next day, for our journey was a long one.

In a way, I think that perhaps those days were the best of any journey that I can remember now.

Between us there was no word of shop or home or work; just the talk of a girl who had read, and read very well, a girl to whom hard experience had given a big sane view of life, a girl who had become a philosopher in her own right. She had been talking to me once of the early French dramatists and the effect they had had on the playwrights of to-day, and her views, like all her views, were at least individual. When she had finished, I looked down at the tip of her shoe.

"Is that the toe of the boot of the well-known dancing soubrette, Alice Abercrombie?" I asked.

"Wait till you see me Wednesday night," she said, "and I'll show you a dance! Much more interesting than Racine, I promise you."

For the greater part of those two days we were by ourselves; but occasionally we received visits from Adler, who forever talked of the stars he had managed and their eccentricities. Marie Belden, the soubrette, and Altha Ryan and Carroll and Baker, too, came into the drawing-room several times; but these visits for the most part were short and productive only of sighs of regret for Broadway and the other haunts of the actors' pet city.

When I awoke on the last morning of our journey I found that the train was side tracked at Prescott; and from my window I could see that the real work of the tour of "The Princess Popinjay" had begun. Long drays were backed up to the cars for the scenery, and heavy express wagons were carting away the costume trunks and crates of properties. Youths whom I had seen lolling about the train or playing poker with the chorus girls had suddenly become galvanized into men of authority, and were quietly but surely bringing order out of what seemed to me the most hopeless chaos. Above it all Ben Adler ruled supreme. One moment he was giving directions as to how to load a particularly heavy piece of scenery, and the next with a Chesterfieldian grace was conducting a show girl to a hotel omnibus. In the midst of it all he seemed to remember me; for he came dashing into the car and knocked on the door of my compartment.

"Don't forget, you are to be the iron magnate to-day," he said. "You'll find a room engaged for you at the Holter House in the name of Henry Speed. Miss Abercrombie will be ready as soon as you are. You're to take her up in a sleigh. It's something of a drive to the town."

I had seen a few Pittsburg millionaires at the Holland House, and could not remember that there was anything particularly distinctive about their dress; but I picked out a particularly lively gray waistcoat with a black tape binding, and with this and a pair of white spats felt that I rather looked the part. Alice Abercrombie joined me, and a moment later we were racing along the country road that led to the town.

"Fine, Alice!" said I. It was the first time that I had called her Alice; but I thought that the conditions excused it.

"Alice!" she repeated, and crinkled her brow and pointed the tips of her mouth in the same inscrutable smile.

"Yes, Alice," I said, and being in a sleigh on a deserted road on a wonderful morning in January, I took her gloved hand in mine, and raising it to my lips kissed the tips of her fingers. The girl slowly withdrew her hand from mine and settled back in the cushions of the sleigh. Her cheeks were flushed with the sharp morning air; but the smile went out of her eyes, and for the rest of our little ride she looked away from me and out at the snow-covered fields.

We separated at the hotel and I went to my room to be interviewed by the reporter of the only evening newspaper. I talked of the Pittsburg art gallery, which I never had seen, and the Pittsburg orchestra, which I never had heard, and even spoke encouragingly of preferred steel, which I never owned; but at mention of the tender mission which brought me to Prescott I blushed, but refused to talk, and with a few laudatory words on the beauty of the town I allowed my reporter friend to depart. Later I went down to the lobby of the hotel, where I found the men of the company sitting about and I asked them into the café, where we drank to the success of the new play. Afterwards I lunched with Carroll and Altha Ryan and for some time we talked as we three had always talked of New York.

"I suppose this amuses you?" Carroll said.

"Of course," I replied; "it's a new story to me. I like the idea of new towns and new faces."

Carroll nodded. "I suppose it was like that to me once; but I can't remember it. New towns don't mean anything to me any more. Do they to you, Altha?"

The girl shook her head.

"There is just a depot," he went on, "and a hotel and an 'opry house,' and then there's another depot and a hotel and an 'opry house.' The people are all alike; they belong to the town, and you don't. You're 'the troupe,' and you come and go like a snow that lasts over one night. The people are nothing to you, and you are nothing to them. If you haven't got friends in the company, Heaven help you!"

"That's right, Jim," said the girl; "it's 'the troupe' or nothing."

"Well," I interrupted, smiling, "personally I like 'the troupe.' I only wish you were all as satisfied as I am."

"Oh, it's all right with you," Carroll said. "You don't really belong to 'the troupe.' You can leave whenever you want to and go back to the white lights of Broadway. Bless them!"

And then Adler came to our table and told Carroll and Miss Ryan to hurry over to the theatre for rehearsal, and I was left alone again to wonder if I was always to be an outsider.

Half-past eight found me seated alone in the upper stage box at the first performance of "The Princess Popinjay" and the first appearance as a star of Miss Alice Abercrombie. From the rise of the first curtain the opera went with a swing and a dash that was extraordinary. Wainwright makes few mistakes, and this time apparently he had left no loop-hole for failure to creep in. In a misty sort of way I can remember Altha Ryan and Baker singing many verses of a duet, and Carroll looking very well in his white duck suit and a sword clashing at his side. Many of the girls, too, whom I had formerly known on the train in shirtwaists and short skirts, I recognized now as wonderfully beautiful daughters of a travelling English millionaire or in the black

tight-fitting dresses of *vendeuses* in a Paris mil-
linery shop.

But what I saw distinctly, and it was what every
one else in that crowded audience recognized, was
the sweeping success of Alice Abercrombie. She, too,
had allowed for no chance of failure. To that performance she had brought the result of years of hard
work and the training of the best masters. To one end
she had toiled unceasingly, breaking down the bar-
riers as she met them, and when the great test came
she rose to it and carried everything before her. It
was at the end of the second act that she achieved her
greatest tirumph. Again and again she was called
before the curtain, until it seemed there would be
no end to it. I looked down from my box at the new
star, and once, I think, she looked up at me; but I
remember that everything was blurred by the direct
rays of the footlights. I turned and stared at the
mass of faces below me, and my one thought was of
myself—that for two days this girl had been quite
alone—alone with me, *with me!*

And then it seemed as if I could stand the noise
no longer, and so I hurried down the staircase that

led from my box to the little door that opened on to the stage. I pushed my way through a crowd of excited, chattering chorus girls and ran up an iron staircase that led to the star's dressing-room. Just outside of this room there was a small platform that extended to the proscenium arch and was used by the man who had charge of the colored lights. The platform was vacant for the moment, and so I walked out on it and peered over the railing, that I might see Miss Abercrombie go before the curtain again.

And then directly back of me I heard her voice. She and Baker were standing on the landing in front of her dressing-room, and while I could see them they did not notice me, because there were several bunchlight stands between us. Apparently she had stopped him on his way to his room on the floor above.

"You'd better go back, little one," I heard him say, and he nodded toward the audience. "They seem to want you out there bad. It sounds good for several calls yet."

And it really sounded to me as if the enthusiasm of the audience was greater than it had been at any time. For a moment she stood there flushed and panting, her big eyes all afire with the excitement of her triumph. After all, this was the moment of her life, for which she had waited and planned so long. There would be other successes and other triumphs; but there could be only one first triumph.

"You'd better take the call," Baker urged, and started on toward his own room; but the girl reached out her white arm and, taking him by the shoulder, swung him back so that he faced her again.

"What do I care about their noise? What do I care about them?" she gasped. "What I want to know is if you love me—me, do you understand, and not that Altha Ryan girl?"

I do not know what Baker said or did, because the hundreds of electric lights all about the stage seemed to flare up suddenly, and I steadied myself by holding tight to the iron railing at my side, and looked away from them and down on the cleared stage.

A few minutes later I knocked at her door, and she told me that I might come in. She was standing in front of her mirror, her knuckles resting on the dressing-table in front of her. As I spoke she did not take her eyes from those in the looking-glass.

"I've come to say good-by," I said; "I have decided to go back to New York. Quite unintentionally I heard you talking just now to Baker. When you said that I didn't belong—that I was only an outsider—I could not understand exactly. That was probably because I didn't want to; but I do now. I am leaving you with your own people. Good-by."

The girl inclined her head very slightly, and I left her just as I had found her, still looking into the mirror.

In a drawer of my desk at home there is a little folder, and on the cover it says, "Tour of the Princess Popinjay Company," and inside there is a list of towns where the company plays and the dates on which it appears in each town. Very often during the best hour of the twenty-four, which I think is between six and seven o'clock in the evening, I take out this card and find out just where "The Princess Popinjay" is that night. I can imagine the chorus girls walking arm in arm through the streets of the little town, unobserving but much observed as members of "the troupe"; down in the hotel office Ben Adler is talking to the clerk; and the actors are sitting with their chairs tilted against the wall; and Baker and Carroll and Altha Ryan and Alice Abercrombie have just come in for dinner after a drive or a stroll through the town. And later I know they will all put on their fine plumage and go through the play, not even knowing the name of the town so well probably as I do; but they will have their jokes and their gossip and their laughter and their hard-luck stories behind the scenes and in the dressing-rooms, and they will be happy in their own way and in their own world.

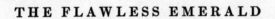

THE FLAWLESS EMERALD

THE FLAWLESS EMERALD

WITH the exception of the adventure I am now about to relate, my life has been conventional, dull, and prosaic. This, I am bound to state, has been no fault of my own, for my spirit is really a most adventurous one, and I am sure that had my lot been that of a gentleman of leisure, instead of a clerk in a cotton house, I should have had such experiences as we are led to believe were common a hundred years ago. Instead of dashing about the world, accompanied by a few kindred spirits, in a rakish black craft and exploring nooks and crannies of the globe yet untouched by the foot of the white man, it has been my fate to divide my life in New York between our office downtown, and comfortable though modest rooms in a bachelor apartment-house on West Twenty-sixth Street. My movements have also been somewhat confined by a hard business sense which I

237

must have derived from my Puritan ancestors—a sense which has given me the reputation of a valued employee, and has inspired a consistent practice of not spending more than two-thirds of my income. As a result, I have never been able to travel very far afield for my romance, and have had to content myself with such adventure as I found in books and on the stage.

I know my New York thoroughly, for I have gone over every quarter of it time and again, always by myself, and usually at night, but it is the land of the money-grubber, not of romance—no gloved hand has ever waved to me from a passing brougham and no fair face has yet appeared at a window of a deserted house. The few experiences I have had on my nocturnal wanderings have always resulted in my hasty flight in order to avoid a street brawl or some equally vulgar proceeding. And so, with a feeling of real regret, I have always been forced to return to my novel at home in my little study or go back to my front seat at the theatre and find my adventures among the people of stage-land.

As in all other cotton houses, our work for the

year is most unevenly divided—for six months we
toil ceaselessly and for the remainder of the time we
have really little or nothing to do. Many of our force
are employed only for the busy season. I, with several others, am engaged for the whole twelve months,
but during the slack season our firm has gladly per-
mitted us to take long vacations on half-pay.

The work during the season just ended had been
particularly severe, and I had decided that I would,
for the first time during the ten years with which I
had been connected with the house, treat myself to
a long vacation. I had determined in a general way
that I should go abroad, but had arranged nothing
definitely farther than that I should spend the first
days of my holiday in absolute idleness in the city
where I had recently worked so hard. I had completed all the pending business at the office, and was
even in the act of shutting down my roller-top desk
with a feeling of genuine relief, when Mr. Arthur
Kellard walked into my office.

Mr. Kellard was an occasional customer of the
house, and frequently came in to consult me in regard to his account. I knew little of him beyond the

facts that he had an office at 120 Broadway, was supposed to have large interests in some Mexican mines,
and to all appearances, was a gentleman forty years
of age and of polite address. On the occasion of which
I speak he asked me about his account, and, having
obtained the required information, he entered into a
conversation on general topics with me. I told him of
my intended vacation and that I was even then about
to take my leave of the office. To this he suggested
that we should walk uptown together and begin my
holiday by taking a drink with him at his club. I
gladly assented, and he interested me greatly on our
way uptown by suggesting various tours I might take
as the best way of spending my vacation.

His club, while not of the very first social impor-
tance, like the Union or Knickerbocker, had a very
good address on Fifth Avenue, and I was soon most
comfortably ensconced in a large leather chair with
a glass of Scotch, a good cigar, and my new friend
across the little table telling me of the possibilities of
European travel. When we entered the room there
were but two other members present. They were sitting at the next window to ours and looking with a

languid interest at the passing show on the Avenue.
Mr. Kellard evidently was not acquainted with them,
as he did not recognize them either when entering
the room or afterward. We sat together for perhaps
half an hour, and then my host begged me to excuse
him, as he had an engagement uptown, but suggested
that I should remain where I was or make myself at
home wherever I chose in the club. I readily acceded
to this suggestion, as I was not a member of any club,
and thoroughly enjoyed the novelty of the situation.

I had been sitting at the window alone for some
minutes, thinking only of the passers-by and the long
lines of fine carriages with their beautifully dressed
owners, and rather hoping that some of my acquaintances might see me in the club window, when my
attention was arrested by a remark made by one of
the two men at the neighboring window. A young and
very pretty girl had just driven by in a runabout. I
had myself noticed her, not only on account of her
beauty, but because of the extreme smartness of the
vehicle and the livery of the little tiger sitting beside
her.

"Nice girl," said one of the men; "but very eccentric, very."

From where I was sitting I could easily hear their conversation and, quite unobserved, get a good look at them. The man who spoke was the elder of the two. He was perhaps forty years of age, extremely well groomed, and his most distinctive feature was a blonde moustache turned up at the ends very much in the style affected by the Emperor William. His friend, who looked to be about thirty years of age, had a clean-shaven face, and, like the other man, had the appearance and manner of a true cosmopolite.

"I have never met her," answered the younger man, "but she always looks most attractive and quite unlike other actresses. For instance, she doesn't crown herself with white plumes and loll back in a .victoria. Did you notice that dress she had on when she passed just now? Her whole appearance was that of a very smart girl in society, and her trap was just as well turned out as herself. I have often thought I should like to meet her."

"I wish we could all have supper together some night after the performance," said the man with the blonde moustache, "but she is most difficult. That is one of her eccentricities. Ada Caldara never makes engagements. She is quite willing to have you meet her at the stage door, but she always reserves the privilege of refusing your invitation at the last moment and going away with some other friend or back home for a quiet supper with her mother. I have seen half a dozen men waiting for her, and she has left them all standing on the sidewalk looking like a lot of fools, and then driven off in a hansom with her maid. It's wonderful how she holds her friends."

"I saw her last spring when she was playing in London at the Shaftesbury," said the younger man. "She was at a supper young Neimeyer gave her at The Princess. She struck me then as being exceptionally good-looking."

"Do you know Neimeyer?" answered the older man. "It was he who gave her the flawless emerald."

"A flawless emerald? I didn't know there was such a thing," said the young man.

"They are very rare," continued the man with the blonde moustache; "many jewellers who have been in the business all their lives have never seen one, and, as a matter of fact, it is the quickest test to tell a real stone from one of the very good imitations they make nowadays—the imitations are always flawless. Didn't you ever hear of the trouble with the Neimeyers about the stone? It's a very good story, but was hushed up over there by young Neimeyer's friends."

In answer the younger man shook his head. His friend turned to look at me, but I anticipated him and continued to look out of the window as if I were quite unconscious of their presence. The older man took out his cigarette-case, lighted a cigarette, and continued:

"About the time young Neimeyer was so devoted to this girl a very distinguished personage arrived in London with one of the most remarkable collections of jewels in the world."

"An Indian prince?" asked the younger man.

"No, better than that," said his friend. "He was a royal personage; a ruler of a small kingdom all of his own. But like a good many modern rulers he was sadly impoverished, and he came to sell some of his family jewels so that he might straighten out his affairs at home. But it seemed he had a most absurd idea of their value, and demanded such exorbitant prices that his mission failed utterly. To make things worse, he lost a great deal of money gambling at one of the fashionable clubs in London, and tried to make it up at the races, and met with the usual result. In a very short time he found himself deeply in debt to his sponsors at the club and the book-makers as well. In his predicament he turned to old man Neimeyer, who you probably know carries on his business of a dealer in antiquities only as a blind, for since Sam Lewis died he is really the greatest usurer in England. He will loan money on anything from a ducal estate to a trained elephant—that is, as long as he gets his fifty per cent. commission. The most valuable single gem the potentate had in his collection was a flawless emerald, probably the best of its kind in the world, and it was this he took to Neimeyer. To make a long story short, he loaned the gem to the money-lender as security, got enough ready cash to pay his debts and returned to his own country to arrange with his Minister of Finance to pile on taxes sufficient to eventually get his flawless emerald out of pawn. He had until the end of a year, which was the time for which it had been loaned to Neimeyer.

"This is where Miss Caldara got into the game. Young Jacob Neimeyer had been showing the girl all kinds of attentions, and I imagine the affair had put him in a rather bad way financially. Whether it was his lack of funds or just sheer madness over his devotion to her, he went to his father's safe one night, took out the flawless emerald, and carried it with the tale of its great value to the lady he loved so well and unwisely. A few days later the old man wanted to show the gem to a friend, and, of course, discovered the loss. As there were only two or three people who knew about the jewel and who had the combination of the safe, the theft was very soon fixed on the son, and the real trouble began. The boy—for that's what he really is—protested that he had only loaned the jewel to Miss Caldara, but the lady thought differently. She claimed that it was a gift. Neimeyer called in his lawyers, and even Scotland Yard was appealed to, and many and strong were the arguments brought to bear on the young actress. They threatened to arrest her as the receiver of stolen goods, but she very naturally contended that her arrest could only follow that of the thief, and Neimeyer, of course, was anxious to keep his son out of jail as well as to avoid the scandal which would follow the exposé of his transaction with the potentate. There were many meetings and stormy interviews between all the parties concerned, but the upshot of it all was that Miss Caldara agreed to return the jewel within the year from the day it was pawned, so that it should be in Neimeyer's safe by the time the royal personage returned to claim his own. In the meantime, she was to have the privilege of wearing it when and how she liked, but, as a matter of fact, few even of her intimate friends have any idea of its value, as the Neimeyers naturally never speak of the incident, and she is not particularly anxious to tell a story which is but little to her credit."

"Does she often wear it?" interrupted the younger man.

"Very seldom," answered his friend. "In fact, I have never seen her use it on the stage. I always wanted to see it 'from the front,' however, and she promised me at supper last evening that she would positively wear it to-night. Why don't you come to the theatre with me? We can see how the jewel looks over the footlights, and if she will take supper afterward we can examine it at close range. It is really worth while—quite a historic gem."

"I'm sorry," replied the younger man, "but I'm going to a dinner dance and you know what that means. I'll probably not get away before one or possibly two o'clock. It's too bad, for I should really like to see the flawless emerald."

"Well, some other time, then," said the older man, and the two friends, as if by mutual consent, finished their drinks and sauntered out of the room.

I must admit that I had listened to the story of the flawless emerald with great interest. I knew nothing of gems and very little of the heroine of the tale, but I had seen her many times on the stage at the Casino, and had always admired her very greatly for her extreme beauty and an apparently indolent grace which was really most attractive. I was glad to learn something of her, and to listen to a story concerning the intimate doings of such people as the poor potentate and the famous money-lender—people who were part of a life of which I had seen nothing and knew but little. My curiosity to see the wonderful emerald was indeed very great, and nothing would have kept me away from the theatre that night. As it was, I had no engagement, and immediately set out for the Waldorf, where I bought a front seat for that night's performance.

I suppose I should have blamed Miss Caldara for her part in the proceedings, but when she made her appearance I could not find it in my heart to do so. She was quite the loveliest person to look at on the stage and seemed to me worthy to wear any gem however rare and valuable. Indeed, when she smiled pleasantly at a gentleman sitting alone in a stage box, and whom I at once recognized as the one who had told the story of the emerald that afternoon at the club, I really envied him greatly. I had several times read of the wonderful collection of jewels Miss Caldara was supposed to possess, and had on several previous visits to the same play noticed some remarkable diamonds she wore, but on this particular night, during the first two acts, she used no jewels of any description, and I almost gave up hope of seeing the famous flawless emerald. It was at the very last of the third act, when Miss Caldara appeared in a white evening dress, that I caught my first glimpse of the jewel which had already caused so much trouble. She wore it at the edge of her corsage, and its size alone, even had it not been a stone of great brilliancy, would have at once attracted the attention of the audience. The emerald appeared to be about an inch square and needed no other jewels to set off its great beauty—indeed, even the mounting was invisible from my seat in the orchestra. It seemed as if every one about me began discussing the stone at once. The lady sitting next to me contended that it was altogether too large to be genuine, but her escort laughed and said something about Miss Caldara's jewels being finer than any ever worn in a box at the Metropolitan Opera House.

I wished that I might tell them all I knew, and it seemed strange that in all that audience only the man sitting alone in the box and I understood how valuable the stone really was. But, of course, I said nothing, and in a few moments the final curtain fell and Miss Caldara and her emerald were shut off

from our view. It so happened that I had never
counted an actor or an actress among my friends,
and so I had never had any occasion to visit the stage
door of a theatre, but nothing could have tempted
me away from the stage door of the Casino on this
particular night. I wanted to see Miss Caldara again,
and, above all, I wanted to see what became of the
admirers who had come to meet her. The whole idea
struck me as most unique and amusing. I followed
the audience out of the theatre, and slowly walked
around the corner and up Thirty-ninth Street toward
Sixth Avenue. There was a long line of hansoms,
broughams, and automobiles stretching for almost an
entire block, and quite a number of people had already collected about the stage entrance. It was
rather dark, but I could easily see that the crowd
was made up of many classes of society. There were
stage-hands in their working clothes, and very smart-
looking young men in evening dress, and many others
of all conditions waiting for friends, or perhaps, like
myself, attracted there purely from a spirit of curiosity. I watched with much interest the almost continuous line of men and women who were in some

way connected with the theatre as they came through the little door leading to the mysterious realms of stage-land. Many of the girls hurried away singly or in little groups, while others joined their friends and dashed away in the hansoms or automobiles, no doubt to gay suppers that awaited them. The scene was full of human interest to me, and although I was considerably jostled and knocked about by the crowd around the door, the half-hour which passed before Miss Caldara finally appeared slipped by most pleasantly.

It occurred to me, however, as a curious fact, that nowhere in the crowd could I see the man who had told the story of the emerald, and who had occupied the box, while, on the other hand, I was sure that I had recognized his friend who had that afternoon begged off from going to the theatre on account of another engagement. However, as the incident could be accounted for in many ways, and as it was none of my affair anyhow, I gave it but a passing thought.

The actress whom I had waited to see at last made her appearance. There was no question as to her identity, and she looked quite as beautiful to me as

The actress at last made her appearance.

she had on the stage. About her shoulders she wore a long opera cloak which only partially concealed a dress such as any lady might wear to an evening party. Accompanied by her maid and looking neither to the right nor to the left, she brushed her way through the crowd and started toward Sixth Avenue, in which direction her carriage was evidently awaiting her. She had perhaps gone some twenty feet beyond the crowd about the door when she uttered a faint cry and turned suddenly to her maid. After a few hasty words the two women started back toward the theatre. Miss Caldara reëntered the stage door, and the maid ran to the corner and started an earnest conversation with a policeman. The actress returned almost immediately with the stage-door man, and began looking about on the ground as if for some lost article. They were joined by the police officer and the maid, and all four commenced to look over the sidewalk. The officer at first glanced carefully over the crowd. Some of the men returned his stare impudently, while others turned their heads and slowly walked away. In a few moments every one who remained knew that a valuable jewel had been lost by Miss Caldara on her way from the stage door to her carriage, and the whole crowd of men joined in the search of the sidewalk, at the same time eying each other with evident suspicion.

I, too, joined in the search, but I knew that it was quite futile; for the flawless emerald was in my overcoat pocket.

In the great excitement of the moment I could not positively state just when it got there, but it was about the time that Miss Caldara uttered the faint scream and turned back to the theatre. I was completely surrounded at the moment, but I distinctly felt something suddenly forced into my outside pocket. I turned my head, but the men standing back of me were all looking at the beautiful actress, and it was impossible to distinguish which of several men was in the best position to have transferred his plunder to me. The situation was at once perfectly apparent: the thief had snatched the case from Miss Caldara and had passed it on to me instead of his confederate. I was sure that the latter had sneaked away with some of the other men, believing that his pal had decided to hold on to the jewel, while the thief, under the impression that he had successfully carried out the transfer, was even then assisting in the search. An enormous crowd gathered almost immediately, and the sidewalk became black with people.

"I should like to search every one of youse," growled the police officer; but the crowd only laughed and went on lighting matches and using them as torches as they continued to scan the pavement.

For one brief moment I thought of giving up the emerald, but then I considered that I was without a single friend in the crowd, and whatever Miss Caldara might think, my action would certainly be regarded as most suspicious by the mob, which I knew would like nothing better than to see me hurried off to the nearest police station. There would be plenty of time later to make the necessary restitution, and I had sufficient wit to know that hasty action in such crises is always conducive to error. The perspiration came out on my forehead in large drops, and actually ran down my face, but I held my head low and went on with the search, gradually, however, working myself away from the point where the crowd was the greatest. The actress, I must admit, met the difficulty as a true lady should, and did little more than direct the search with decision and without any vulgar display of emotion. I cannot say as much for the maid, who dived about under everybody's legs looking for the jewel-case, in the meanwhile weeping and bewailing the great loss of her mistress.

What eventually occurred and how the crowd was finally dispersed, I do not know; for as soon as I had worked myself to the outer edge of the mob, I sauntered slowly down Thirty-ninth Street and turned into the crowded sidewalks of Broadway. All my life I had been looking for adventure, and when at last it came I cannot say that I found very much pleasure in it—indeed, my only feeling was worse than that of the culprit who is lucky enough to have escaped with his plunder. I walked along the street for several blocks in a semi-dazed condition, my hand in my pocket closely grasping the jewel-case. But the cool night air finally brought me to my senses, and I decided that I must go home and, in the quiet of my own apartment, plan for future action.

THE FLAWLESS EMERALD

The apartment which I occupied was on the second floor and ran the entire length of the building, which was formerly a private residence, but had been recently changed to a combination business and apartment-house. The basement and lower floor were used as shops, and there was but one apartment above my own. As the latter was not rented at the time, and as there was no elevator and the caretaker only came in during the day, I was quite alone in the building after the shops had been closed for the night. I did not care particularly for the arrangement, but I had the satisfaction of knowing that it was not the kind of house which a burglar would care to take the risk of entering, as the shops dealt in only the cheapest kind of goods and my own apartment was simplicity itself. On the present occasion, however, I must confess to a feeling of very great pleasure as I opened the door into my little sitting-room. Here, at least, I was safe with my treasure and free to consider how best to return it to its owner. I took off my hat and overcoat and put the precious case, which I knew must contain the emerald, on my writing desk. I lighted my pipe, and, drawing up a chair, opened the jewel-case. The great green stone lay on a piece of white velvet—from its every facet it shone and sparkled splendidly even in the dull yellow light of my room. I took it out of the case and held it up before the gas-jet—it was as clear as crystal, not the trace of a flaw anywhere. And then I heard the door of the bed-room which was back of me creak on its hinges, and I knew that I was not alone.

My first instinct was to cry aloud for help, but the childish fear which possessed my senses passed as quickly as it had overtaken me, and I laid the jewel on the desk in front of me. There was no possible escape: the windows were closed and heavily cur-tained, and the spring lock of the door had snapped behind me when I entered. My mind seemed to be perfectly clear, but as I listened to the quiet footfalls of some one approaching toward the back of my chair, I was quite conscious that my heart was not beating. I had no• weapon in my desk, and my eyes cast about for something with which I might defend myself, but I saw nothing. There are some sensations which without any previous experience we seem to feel instinctively: for the first time in my life I was conscious of having a pistol held very close to my head. I turned slowly, and my eyes followed the barrel of a revolver up to a white shirt-cuff, the sleeve of a tweed suit, and then to a face partially concealed by a black mask. Holding the revolver very close to my forehead, the man reached out with his free hand, took the emerald, and dropped it into his coat pocket.

"Now, young man," he said, with the revolver still held in very close proximity to my head, "take a piece of that note-paper and write what I tell you."

I was completely in his power, and so I took out the paper and wrote as the thief dictated. This is what I was forced to write: "I hereby swear that this night I have been in full possession of the flawless emerald which belongs to Miss Ada Caldara."

"Now write the date," the burglar said, "and sign the note with your full name."

I did as I was told, and the man picked up the paper and stuck it in the pocket where he had already placed the emerald. Then he backed toward the door.

"Young man," he said, when he had found the door knob, "my advice to you is not to move. If you do I may get it pretty bad if I'm caught, but you'll get the worst of it whatever happens." He spoke with great authority, and even before he had opened the door and backed slowly out I was convinced that there was much truth in his argument. If I ran to the window and called the police, and if they came in time to catch the culprit, which was most doubtful at that time of night and in that neighborhood, I could only accuse the man of stealing a gem which after all had come into my own possession under the most suspicious circumstances. Thus I argued with myself until I heard my front door close with a bang. Then I jumped up, threw open the window and looked out; but the street was apparently deserted and I heard no footsteps to mar the stillness of the night. I returned to my desk, relighted my pipe, and pondered long over my loss—or rather that of Miss Caldara—and just how great was my responsibility in the matter. I know that I cursed the day I had ever heard of the flawless emerald. Here I was, about to set out on my first long vacation abroad, suddenly confronted with the unpleasant facts that I had been the receiver of stolen goods, and that I had then been deprived of the same goods in a most ignominious manner, by an extraordinary burglar, who, not content with his swag, must force me to give him a sworn statement that it had once been in my possession. This was surely no ordinary "second-story" worker, for in no way did he conform to the general idea of the type. His clothes were well cut, his linen was of the finest, and his voice was apparently that of a man of culture. Of course, I know that many men of refinement have become burglars, and the value of the prize in this case was worthy of the best of rogues, but I could not imagine what he wanted with that carefully worded statement. Admitting that I had written myself down a thief, of what possible use could my caller in the black mask make of it? My only satisfaction was in the thought that I was really not guilty, and that while I had been robbed with ridiculous ease, no one, however brave, could have acted differently. My position was a most unfortunate one, and after thinking for a long time over the matter I reached the conclusion that if the law did not prevent, I would still take my vacation abroad and the incidents of that evening should hasten rather than retard my departure. In fact, I decided that the next steamer to leave the port of New York was the best boat for me. Fortunately I had that morning's *Herald* in my room, and I eagerly scanned the shipping news to find if there were a ship sailing the next morning. There was only one, and it was bound for Naples and Genoa.

I had often wanted to visit Italy, the home of romance and adventure, and here was my opportunity. By this time, however, I had convinced myself that I had no choice in the matter, and so I determined to positively sail the next morning. I went into my bedroom to begin my preparations for departure, and for the first time observed how the burglar had entered my apartment. He had not even taken the trouble to close the window leading to the fire-escape, up which he had evidently climbed from the court below. Having reached the platform of the fire-escape, nothing could be easier than to enter the bedroom, as the window was usually open, and even when closed had no safety catch. The apartments in my neighborhood were never built for burglars. Or, perhaps, I should say were built expressly for them.

As my boat did not sail until noon the next day,

THE FLAWLESS EMERALD

I had plenty of time to do my packing, buy my ticket, take out a modest letter of credit, and at such odd moments as I could find run through the morning papers for any news concerning the loss of Miss Caldara's emerald.

All of them mentioned the fact that the actress had been robbed of a valuable jewel on her way from the stage door to her brougham; some treated the matter most seriously and devoted much space to the details, while others referred to the incident but briefly and with a tinge of suspicion. But I at least knew that this was not the imaginings of a press agent but a bona-fide robbery—two robberies in fact.

My emotions, as I leaned over the rail and watched the steamship back out of the slip, were indeed of a curious mixture. Had it not been for the unfortunate incident of the emerald, my feelings would have been simply those of elation at the prospect of visiting Italy, which I always had longed to see, but as it was I felt that I was leaving my own dear country under a cloud—a cloud the dimensions and blackness of which might greatly increase before I even reached Naples. My love for romance and adventure seemed to have been entirely eradicated from my system by the events of the night previous. These and many other unpleasant thoughts whirled through my brain as I watched the tiny waves lapping at the side of the great black boat, and I finally turned away from my place at the rail with a heavy heart. I had walked but a few steps along the deck when I came face to face with the younger of the two men I had seen the day before at the club.

I must say that he was apparently as much surprised at the meeting as myself, and his face showed his feelings plainly. At that instant I knew in my heart that he had been associated in some way with the robbery of the flawless emerald. I was sure of it. He knew its great value, he had been at the stage door when the gem was stolen, and he was, like myself, a passenger on board the first steamer to leave New York after the robbery. I walked up the deck, and then turning, followed him at a considerable distance. Unsuspected, I at last saw him go into a deck state-room. Then I sat down on somebody's steamer chair and waited. When the bugle blew for lunch I took my stand near the gangway, and, having seen him pass safely into the dining-saloon, I started at once for his state-room. The door was open, and the whole place was strewn with the morning and early editions of the evening papers. I entered and found, as I suspected, that every paper was open at the page whereon appeared the story of Miss Caldara's loss. I was convinced then that on board of the very same boat as myself was the flawless emerald, and, in all probability, the thief himself. Of the latter fact I was not at all sure—there was a certain general similarity between the man on the boat and the one who had robbed me of the gem, but I could not quite establish any particular point of resemblance.

During the voyage I saw very little of Norman Vanvoorst, for that was the name of the man whom I believed to have possession of the emerald. He did not seem to care to associate with his fellow-passengers, and either remained in his cabin or sat alone on the deck, reading such books of travel as the ship's library afforded. For hours and hours I paced the deck, trying to figure out in my own mind the true mystery of the robbery, and if there were no possible way by which I could regain the stone from my fellow-passenger. It was useless to visit his cabin, for if he were the present possessor of the emerald it was quite certain that he either carried it on his person or had given it to the purser for safe-keeping. One thing which led me to the former belief was a peculiarity he had of occasionally feeling for something in his clothes just over his heart, or about where the upper pocket of his waistcoat would be. Often as I watched him sitting in his steamer chair or walking along the deck I saw his hand steal to the same spot over his heart, and in time I became convinced that it was here that he carried the emerald. The easiest solution of the robbery, so it seemed to me, was that Vanvoorst had heard of the almost priceless jewel at a time when he was in great need of money, that he had gone to the stage door on that eventful night, and had watched his confederate, who was probably a practised pick-pocket, steal the jewel-box from Miss Caldara and by mistake pass it to me instead of to himself. The error once made, there was nothing to do but follow me to my home and rob me in the masterly fashion which one of them most certainly accomplished. Of one thing I am convinced, and that was that long before we reached Gibraltar I had lost all sense of fear for my own part in the robbery and thought only of revenge and the possibility of getting the emerald from Vanvoorst, and in due time returning it to its rightful owner. But I could devise no means to accomplish these ends—to have tried to take the jewel back by main force would have been madness, and I should only have been put in irons for my trouble. But on one point I was quite determined. Wherever Vanvoorst left the boat I should leave too, and follow him as long as my resources lasted.

We remained fellow-passengers until we reached Genoa, when it became necessary for both of us to land, as this was the last stop the boat made. When he sent his luggage to the railroad station, I sent my porter after his, and when he had his trunks registered for Monte Carlo, I sent mine after them. I shall always remember that day, as the train jolted its way along the coast through a perfect garden of tropical plants. The deep blue of the sky, the sea a rainbow of color, and the gray rocks covered with myriads of gorgeous flowers gave me a new-born love of nature, and for the time I forgot that there ever had been such a person as Miss Caldara, or such a gem as the flawless emerald, or that Mr. Norman Vanvoorst occupied a compartment in the same car as my own.

It was late in the afternoon when we arrived at Monte Carlo, and I waited on the station platform until I saw Vanvoorst get into the omnibus from the Hôtel de Paris. I followed in a carriage with my luggage, and was soon most comfortably settled in a large bright room overlooking the sea. There was little probability of my man leaving the place that evening, and so I determined to devote the night to my own amusement. After a good dinner I went over to the Casino, a resort which I had long wished to see, and although I understood but little of the games of roulette or trente-et-quarante, I found the scene a most diverting one. I had been wandering about from table to table for perhaps half an hour, when there was a sudden and to me inexplicable stampede toward one of the rooms at the farther end of the building, where the trente-et-quarante tables were situated. I hurried along with the crowd, and as I passed two men, who were evidently English, I heard one of them say to the other: "Hurry up—old Neimeyer is trying to break the bank."

This indeed was good luck for me. I had not only always wanted to see the bank at Monte Carlo broken, but I most certainly wanted to see the man who was going to do it, especially if he were the Neimeyer who had once possessed the flawless emerald. By the time I reached the trente-et-quarante room, the place was crowded to the point of suffocation. It was impossible to make my way through the dense mob surging about the table, so I climbed on one of the velvet lounges and had a fine view of the whole proceeding. Mr. Neimeyer looked about sixty years of age, was short and stout, and quite bald. Of all the immense crowd in the big room he seemed to be the only one who had not temporarily gone mad. He sat at the side of the table, half-way between the croupiers, and as each time he put down the maximum bet of twelve thousand francs and waited for the cards to be dealt, he smiled and chatted pleasantly with the croupiers. When he won, and it seemed as if he could not lose, his little eyes twinkled and he folded up his winnings and stuck the notes deep in his inside pocket. During the few plays I saw him make the excitement in the room was intense, for, as I afterward learned, it is considered a most difficult feat to break the bank at trente-et-quarante. The finish came very quickly and, at least to me, most unexpectedly. Neimeyer had as usual bet the maximum and as usual won. The chief croupier opened the lid of his brass-bound money-chest, looked into it and then across the table at Neimeyer, smiled pleasantly and nodded his head. Then with one of the croupier's rakes, he rapped on the bell lying in the centre of the table, which was the sign for one of the attendants to bring another chest of money. At the sound of the bell the crowd broke into a loud cheer, and in the general confusion that followed I asked an Englishman standing near who it was that had broken the bank, and he told me it was Neimeyer, the famous antiquity dealer from London. I was glad, for I felt that before I left Monte Carlo I probably should need his services and that he possibly might need mine.

When the rooms had been closed for the night I followed the crowd out of the Casino, and with many others crossed the road to the café opposite. In that scene of gayety I must admit that I felt most lonely and miserable. I would have given much for the sight of the face of a friend, or even an acquaintance, with whom I could have had a good-night drink. I sat alone at a table near the wall and listened to the Hungarian band and watched the merry-makers about me. Not twenty feet from me Vanvoorst sat at a table with two very smart-looking women and a man, who were evidently old friends. I noticed that they continually glanced up at the Casino clock, and after perhaps half an hour the whole party arose and started in the direction of the railway station. It was evident that Vanvoorst's friends were stopping at Nice or Cannes and had come down to Monte Carlo to dine and spend the evening with him. Now he was going to accompany them to the station and would probably return alone. I paid my check and then followed them at a safe distance through the gardens. I saw them go down the hill, but I remained on a rocky terrace overlooking the sea. I heard the Nice train arrive and depart, and then I retraced my steps to a turn in the path where the garden seemed to be the most isolated and the foliage the thickest. I stood behind some bushes, where the leaves completely hid me from view, and waited for the return of my man. I saw him slowly walking up the path—he was smoking and completely unconscious that he was being watched. As he reached a point opposite the bushes behind which I had been concealed, I stepped out in the middle of the path and confronted him. For a moment there was silence, while I looked him full in the eyes, and he in return regarded me with a look of the most languid interest.

"Well?" he said at last.

"You have," I answered, "in your possession an emerald, the property of Miss Ada Caldara, which you stole or had stolen from me. You are going to give it to me, and you are going to give it to me now."

"That," said Vanvoorst, "is, I regret to say, not the case. I have not got Miss Caldara's emerald about me, and if you crossed the ocean in the hope of regaining it, you have made a serious mistake, for the stone is still in New York. Will you now kindly let me pass or are you going to try to go through my clothes? I should not advise you to try the latter plan, as you would probably be interrupted by a guard, and you possibly know that the laws over here for foreign criminals are most complicated."

"It is possible," I answered, "that you have not the emerald with you at this moment, but when you say it is not in Monte Carlo you lie. There is another here who has a greater interest in that particular jewel than myself, and he is very powerful and very rich, and with his aid I will yet defeat you. On the steamer you carried the emerald in your upper waistcoat pocket over your heart. I know that it is not there now, but it is not far away, and, be sure, I will not lose sight of you until I have recovered it."

I stepped aside, and Vanvoorst sauntered on his way to the hotel. Once again I had been made a fool of and accomplished nothing, except that the man had practically admitted his knowledge of the robbery of the emerald. I returned to my room tired and discouraged, and as I lay in bed I decided that if no device occurred to me on the morrow whereby I could recover the emerald, I should go to Neimeyer, tell him the whole story, and ask for his aid, which under the circumstances, I did not see how he could well refuse.

The next day I spent in the gambling rooms, for the most part watching Vanvoorst lose at roulette. He played a reckless game, and, as the luck seemed to be all against him, his losses must have been very heavy. After he had lost all the French money he had with him, he took out of his pocket-book some American bank-notes and sent an attendant to have them changed into French money. He continued to play with this for some time, but his bad luck would not leave him, and he finally lost his last gold piece. With a gesture of disgust, he left the table and hurried from the room. I had been sitting across the table, and, in order to hold my position, had been making some modest wagers on the game, of which by this time I had picked up a fairly good understanding. As I had been playing in direct opposition to Vanvoorst, I was a good winner, and was loath to quit playing, although I had a presentiment that should have kept me from letting him for a moment out of my sight. I continued to play for perhaps half an hour, when my luck changed, and after losing a part of my winnings I got up from the table and went out of the Casino for a breath of fresh air. Just as I reached the steps

THE FLAWLESS EMERALD

I saw Neimeyer some distance off, and walking in the direction of the Galerie Charles III. With no definite purpose, I followed him and saw him enter the Galerie and stroll slowly along, stopping frequently to look into the windows of the little shops. I think it is the third one from the entrance that is occupied by a jeweller, and as I slowly followed Neimeyer I noticed that the window was full of the most beautiful gems and the finest specimens of the goldsmith's art. As I afterward learned, it is a shop most liberally patronized by those who have lost their money at the gaming-tables, and must necessarily sell their jewels or valuables to recoup their depleted fortunes. There were certainly some very remarkable jewels in the window on this occasion, and the prices seemed to be particularly moderate. I glanced over the different articles, and was about to turn away and continue my walk up the Galerie, when my eye fell on a jewel which I at once knew I had seen before. It was the flawless emerald. Like many of the other jewels, it was pinned to a white card on which were written the words "Occasion—12,000 fr." To be sure that there was no mistake, I went into the shop and asked to examine the jewel more closely. I held it up to the light, and it was without a flaw. In addition to this there could be no mistaking the color, the shape, and the cutting. It was evident that Vanvoorst had sold the emerald. At last I had found the jewel I sought, but the price placed it as far beyond my reach as it had ever been. Much as I wanted the stone back, I could not afford twelve thousand francs. I left the shop and walked down to the end of the Galerie, where I found Mr. Neimeyer sitting on the balustrade looking out on that wonderful picture of rocks and sea. My mind was already made up, and I approached the money-lender and introduced myself. He received my advances pleasantly and made a few conventional remarks about the view which lay before us.

"I know, Mr. Neimeyer," I said, "that you are a connoisseur and a recognized authority on the beautiful things of this world, and there is something in the window of a little shop on the Galerie of which I wish to ask your opinion. Could you so far oblige me?"

Mr. Neimeyer smiled his assent, and together we walked to the jeweller's window.

"Do you see that emerald?" I asked, and watched closely the expression of his face. "It is flawless," I continued, "and you know that flawless emeralds of that size are exceedingly rare. The price, twelve thousand francs, seems very small?"

The old man showed but a polite interest in the emerald, and his manner, I must confess, annoyed me greatly.

"The fact," he said, "that the price is small has really little bearing on its value. Strictly speaking, this is not a pawn-shop, but the owner buys jewels outright from people who need the money very badly and sells them again at what he considers a legitimate profit. I should say it is no doubt an excellent place to find bargains, and this emerald very possibly may be one. Personally, I know nothing of jewels. I am— at least, so they say—an authority on antiquities, but I have never wasted my time over gems any more than I have over ceramics. To understand either of these subjects a man must devote his whole life to it. I hadn't the time, and so when they came in my way I hired an expert to give me their true value."

"Then I am to understand," I said, "that you have never owned a famous flawless emerald?"

The old man regarded me curiously with his beady eyes. "No," he answered, "never. Was that what you wished to know?" he added.

"Thank you, yes," I said, "and I will not trouble you further." I raised my hat, the old man smiled in return, and I turned on my heel and walked slowly up the path. He was either a very truthful old gentleman or a consummate actor, and I chose to believe the latter.

"Twelve thousand francs," I repeated again and again as I walked up the hill. In my pocket I had something over two thousand francs. The English bank and the Crédit Lyonnais were closed for the day, and even had they been open my letter of credit was hardly equal to the emergency. Half-way to the hotel I stopped and looked up at the yellow walls of the Casino. Through the open windows I could hear the droning voices of the croupiers and the ceaseless chink of the gold and silver pieces. Within, I knew that the tables were covered with them, and in the vaults below were many, many millions, and yet I stood there impotent and routed, and only twelve thousand francs between myself and victory.

"Black, black," I said to myself over and over again, as I hurried on to the door of the Casino. I walked to the first roulette table and put my two thousand francs on the black.

"Dix, noir, pair et manque," called the croupier.

I left the money on the table and saw the little marble once more fall into a black pocket. Some one shoved two one-thousand-franc notes toward me and left the remaining six on the color. For one moment I tried to say "Rouge," but my throat was parched and the same voice inside of me kept on whispering "Black, black." "Vingt-six, noir, pair et passe," sang out the croupier. I had played the maximum and won. I gathered up the notes and stuck them deep into my trousers pocket. "I win! I win!" I said to myself as I hurried out of the Casino and started on a run for the Galerie. For a moment I paused to glance into the window of the jeweller's. The emerald was gone!

I rushed into the shop. "There was," I gasped, "an emerald in your window."

"Yes," said the woman behind the counter, "we sold it but a few moments since."

"Of course," I answered, "to a friend of mine, an old man, very short and stout, and with a Jewish face."

The woman nodded and smiled. "It was a great bargain, I think," she said, "but we had a rare opportunity to buy it very cheap."

Once more I climbed the hill, but I did not stop to listen at the open windows of the Casino. I went to my room in the hotel and threw myself on the bed. I was tired and discouraged, and decided to take my leave on the morrow—never again did I want to see Monte Carlo or Vanvoorst or Neimeyer. To be sure, the latter had but come into his own, and I should have been satisfied, but a pain about my heart told me that it was not as I would have had it. In all my dealings with the flawless emerald it appeared, after all, that my interest had been solely inspired by a desire in some way to assist Miss Caldara. And now I was defeated in my hunt, and she would never know how very hard I had toiled on her behalf, and the smile and the word of thanks with

"I put my money on the black."

which I had hoped to be rewarded were never to be mine.

By the next morning I had decided to take the first train for Genoa and from there to go on a short tour of Italy. I packed my trunk, paid my bill at the hotel, and started for the station. Arriving there, I discovered that there had been an accident on the road, and that my train would be at least an hour late. I left my luggage at the station and walked up the hill to have one more look at the gaming-tables, although I was determined not to give back any of my winnings. I left my hat and overcoat at the cloak-room and stopped for a moment to speak to the flower-girl, who had smilingly offered me a boutonnière. I turned my head, and at my right saw Neimeyer waiting to give his things to the attendant. From his inside pocket he took a fat-looking pocket-book, and, having extracted all the bank-notes it contained, stuck it back in the pocket of his overcoat and handed the latter to one of the girls who was taking care of the wraps. As she gave him the brass coat-check, I heard her say in French, "Thirty-four, a lucky number. I wish you success with it." Neimeyer smiled and bustled on toward the gambling rooms. I was quite sure that he did not have the emerald with him, and having considered the matter the evening previous, I was equally sure that it was deposited in the safe in the hotel office as it was hardly possible that he would leave so valuable an article in his room. If the emerald was in the safe at the hotel, then the receipt in all probability was in the big pocket-book. In any case, it seemed worth the chance; so I went into the room and found the money-lender playing his usually heavy game at trente-et-quarante. I returned to the cloak-room, and, carefully picking out one of the attendants who had not waited on Neimeyer, made a great pretence of looking for my hat-check.

"It was number thirty-four," I said, "but I seem to have lost it."

The woman smiled politely, but without apparent interest in my loss. I took out a five-franc piece and said that I was very considerably pressed for time. Again the woman smiled politely and said that I had probably left it on the table where I had been playing. I took a louis out of my pocket and said that if she could let me have my things it would be a great convenience.

"It is very irregular," she said, as she handed me Neimeyer's coat and hat, "and if you find the check I hope that you will return it."

I think I said that I would, but did not waste very much time in formalities. Once out of the Casino, I hurriedly looked through Neimeyer's papers, and among the first I discovered was the receipt for a package left at the hotel. I held the paper in my hand and walked hurriedly up to the clerk at the hotel desk.

"Mr. Neimeyer," I said, "is having a rather bad run of luck at the rooms and he sent me over for this package," and I gave the clerk the receipt. The clerk was apparently used to such hurry calls for money and suspected nothing. My only fear was that the package might look as if it did not contain bank-notes, but the sight of a long white envelope relieved me of all my fears. I left the hotel on a run for the Casino, but once outside, I stopped to tear open the envelope. It contained a plain white jewellers' box, and in the box lay the emerald. I returned to the

Casino, deposited Neimeyer's hat and coat with the pocket-book in the pocket in which I had originally found it. Then I went upstairs to the writing-room, put twelve thousand francs in an envelope, addressed it to Neimeyer at the Hôtel de Paris, stamped and mailed it, and, having taken out my own hat and coat, walked down to the station and waited for the train. I believe I actually did not have to walk up and down the platform of that railway station for over fifteen minutes, but it seemed to me an eternity. Even when once started, I knew that there was an excellent chance of being stopped, and I also knew that in the next hour I should have crossed the boundary line of three countries, and that the authorities of Monaco did not care to mix in international legal complications where it possibly could be avoided. My greatest fear of detection was at Genoa, and so I remained in my compartment and was carried on to Pisa.

From Pisa I hurried on the same night to Leghorn, where, as I had hoped, I found a vessel belonging to one of the smaller steamship lines about to start for New York. I might have taken a chance and remained in the country, but I cannot say that my mind was much attuned to sightseeing, and so I left Italy a fugitive from justice just as a few weeks before I had left my own country. Whatever had happened in America since my departure in regard to the robbery of the emerald I did not know or care. Now I was in a position to make full reparation for a crime I had never committed, and, with the flawless emerald stuck deep down in my inside pocket, I feared nothing.

My return voyage to America was long and unpleasant, but, once back in my old rooms in New York, my first act was to write Miss Caldara a note asking for an interview which I assured her would be of great mutual benefit. The next morning I received my answer, and that same afternoon I found myself most comfortably ensconced in a deep chair in Miss Caldara's Louis Quinze drawing-room and ready to tell my story of the lost emerald.

Indeed, I could not have wished it otherwise; the white-and-gold room was filled with great masses of flowers and plants, and the whole place was aglow with the orange light of the setting sun. Miss Caldara and I sat on opposite sides of a cosey little tea-table, and the fact that she told the maid that she was at home to no one did not at all detract from my happiness.

"You have come, no doubt," began Miss Caldara, "to tell me of all your troubles in connection with that awful emerald."

"I have," I answered, "but I was not aware that you knew of my connection with the affair."

The actress smiled most pleasantly upon me. "I fear, I know," she said, "much more than you suspect, and if you will permit me I shall claim a woman's privilege and tell my story first."

"I should be delighted," I said, and sank deeper down in my chair with a feeling of real relief that I had not yet told her that at that very moment I had the emerald in my inside pocket.

"Not so very long ago," began Miss Caldara, "it really seems but yesterday, I was given a very handsome emerald."

I smiled and made some remark to the effect that I was not wholly ignorant of its existence.

"A short time after I had received the gift," con-

tinued Miss Caldara "I had a little supper party
here in my rooms to which I had invited Mr. Arthur
Kellard, Mr. Norman Vanvoorst, both of whom I
believe you know, and a Mr. Scott, whom I do not
think you have ever met. Mr. Vanvoorst is really a
very remarkable young man. He comes of an old
family and most unfortunately inherited a great deal
of money. Had such not been the case it is quite certain that he would have made an enviable career for
himself in any profession which he chose to adopt.
As it is, he has devoted his life to jeunes filles dances,
and dinner parties, with occasional relapses of tiger-
hunting in India, and more or less successful attempts
to break automobile records on circular tracks. He is
absolutely without fear, and is constantly trying to
find a new sensation; he is the best of talkers, and in
an argument insists on taking the wrong side and
always forming himself into the opposition. On the
occasion of the little supper party which I mentioned,
the subject of my recently acquired emerald and my
other jewels came up for discussion. I contended that
we should not really be allowed the responsibility of
owning such valuable jewels, as for the most part

women were extremely careless, and the only wonder to me was that the robbery of valuable gems was so very rare. Of course, Vanvoorst took the opposite side and claimed that women were not at all careless, and that the whole method of life of a woman rich enough to own valuable jewels was a complete fortification against robbers. 'Everything,' he said, 'to-day is for the rich people and against the poor burglar—the private bank vaults, the safe at home, the private detective in the theatre and at all the large functions, and the maid with a pedigree of references a yard long form a network around my lady's jewels which makes them about as safe as if they were still undug from the rocks in which they were formed. All one has to do to prove my point is to look over the police records—there is hardly a case of the successful robbery of valuable jewels. And it is for this that I have lost all patience with the professional burglar. He spends all of his time scheming to steal only the most valuable jewels or trying to break into a bank, and he generally gets a long sentence for his pains when he might have devoted the same time to robbing the fairly well-to-do class, made a comfortable

THE FLAWLESS EMERALD

living, and without any particular danger of arrest The middle classes know that the burglar cares really only for the very rich, and as a consequence they are absolutely unprepared for any attack on such goods as they may possess. For instance, I cannot conceive of any possible way of depriving you of your emerald, but granted that it has passed into the hands of any one who is not accustomed to the possession of articles of value, and I will guarantee to deprive him of it within an hour from the time he first laid hands on it.'

"A general argument followed, and the two men took sides with Mr. Vanvoorst against me. To make a long story short, the talk resulted in a wager in which I bet Mr. Vanvoorst he could not willingly get back my emerald in an hour from the time it had come into another's possession. Of course the great difficulty was to select the person to give it to. We discussed many young men of our acquaintance, and had about decided on a clerk in Mr. Kellard's office when the latter suddenly thought of yourself, whom he seems to have known fairly well in a business way, and you were selected for the victim."

By this time I had recovered my composure, and I found sufficient voice to ask Miss Caldara some leading, but as I thought pertinent, questions.

"And then as I understand it," I said, "I was decoyed to the club to listen to the story of the flawless emerald with the sole object of slipping me the jewel at the stage door."

Miss Caldara smiled sympathetically. "Rather ingenious of Vanvoorst, was it not?" she said.

"And it was he who later robbed me?" I asked.

"Quite so," answered the actress. "You see, he found out that the apartment over your own was not occupied, so he got the keys from the agent on the pretence that he wanted to show them to a friend late in the evening, and on the promise of returning them the following morning. After he had slipped the emerald into your pocket at the stage door he took an automobile to your house, let himself into the vacant apartment and came down to your room by way of the fire-escape. It was really quite a vindication of his theory, wasn't it?" Miss Caldara smiled sweetly.

"It was," I said, "and I hope he won his wager.

He even had the documentary evidence to prove his victory."

"Oh, yes," answered Miss Caldara, "but owing to your delay in reaching your apartment that night it was a question whether he really stole the jewel within the stipulated time. When, however, he had returned to my place after having relieved you of the stone, and we had all thoroughly gone over the terms of the wager, it turned out that in any case I had lost on a simple technicality."

"You interest me greatly," I said, somewhat facetiously.

"You see," ran on Miss Caldara, "by the terms of the agreement, I was to give him the emerald immediately after I left the stage that night, so that he could pass it on to you, but just before starting for the theatre I weakened, left the real emerald at home and took only the imitation in its place."

"The imitation?" I gasped.

"Yes," replied Miss Caldara. "You know that nearly every actress has exact imitations made of her jewels to wear on every-day, or, I should say, every-night, occasions."

"Then the jewel which was stolen from me that night," I asked, "was not the famous flawless emerald which young Neimeyer had given you?"

"It was a fine, flawless piece of green glass," said the actress, smiling; "and young Neimeyer never gave me anything. In fact, I never met the gentleman. That was an additional and, at least it seemed to me, unnecessary fiction on the part of Mr. Vanvoorst to make sure that you would go to the theatre."

"Then if I understand you aright," I said, "you really did once own some sort of an emerald which somebody gave you, and both it and its imitation were in your possession after your robber friend Vanvoorst had returned here that night with the imitation stone which he took from me."

"Of course," said Miss Caldara. "Very lucky for me, wasn't it?"

"Very," I answered. "And have you got them yet?"

"Certainly," said the actress. "The original is in a vault at the bank and the imitation is in the next room." Miss Caldara smiled in very joy of her possessions, and my fingers unconsciously stole to the package in my pocket containing the emerald I had stolen from old Neimeyer.

"But why," I said, "did your friend Vanvoorst go abroad immediately after the robbery?"

"That was quite natural," answered the actress. "He had decided to sail on that date some time previous to the night we made the wager, and we fixed the date of the robbery to suit the sailing. I suppose you thought it was just the other way. I got a letter from Vanvoorst last week, and he told me that he had had the pleasure of meeting you in the Casino gardens at Monte Carlo. He also told me to be sure to tell you, in case I should meet you, that he has had the silver suspender-buckle fixed which gave you both so much uneasiness. It seems the points of the clasp were constantly sticking into him just over his heart and under his upper waistcoat pocket. I wonder if I have delivered the message properly? Perhaps I had better show you his letter."

"Please don't disturb yourself," I begged. "I am sure you have delivered the message perfectly."

"That's good," said Miss Caldara; "and now I

am going to have another cup of tea, and you can tell me your story."

I sat for some moments looking across the little table at a beautiful face crowned by great masses of golden hair. For a brief space I closed my eyes, and with the incredible swiftness of dreams my thoughts went back to that senseless voyage to Italy, and the heavy-scented flowers in the room seemed to recall to me those unhappy days at Monte Carlo. How I hated it all! And yet how different it all might be— to go back to those gardens, not in search of a flawless emerald, but just for rest with the full spirit of content—to go back, not alone, but with one so beautiful as——

"Well?" said Miss Caldara. The maid had left the room; we were alone again.

"My story," I said, "seems to begin about where yours left off. It is even then quite a long story, and I fear it is near the time for you to go to the theatre. I think we had better postpone it until another day, and when, perhaps, I know you a little better. I should like very much, however, before I go, to see your emerald."

Miss Caldara went into another room and brought back a leather case. From it she took a jewel and handed it to me.

"This is only the imitation," she said; "the real one, unfortunately, is at the bank. Do you recognize it? You should, for it was once yours for a whole hour."

I took from my pocket the emerald I had brought from Monte Carlo and laid the two stones side by side on Miss Caldara's writing-table. In size and in the cutting they were almost identical, the only variance being in the mounting of the gold clasp at the back, and even in this there was but little difference.

"You must know a great deal about gems," I said. "What do you think of this one?"

The actress looked at it curiously for some time and then held it up to the light.

"It's quite flawless," she said. "They make the imitations so well nowadays that only an expert can distinguish the good from the bad; at least I know I cannot tell the difference. This may be worth a great fortune, and it may be a piece of glass. It is certainly one or the other—any jeweller can tell you."

"Whatever it is," I said, "I travelled a long way to get it, and the only thought I ever had was to bring it back to you."

Miss Caldara looked up at me and smiled, and in answer shook her head.

"You are very good," she said, "but some day there will be a girl who will have a right to it, and then you might be sorry that you had given it to me. I hope that it is really a flawless emerald, and that she will be worthy of it."

And so the stone lies to-day in a drawer in the room in which I was once so ignominiously robbed, and I fear, will continue to lie there unless some one should again choose to visit me by way of the fire-escape. Whether it is worth a fortune, or whether it is a piece of green glass, I really do not know, for I have never shown it to any one. I often, however, take it out and look at it late at night and when I am alone. I value it greatly, not for its possible intrinsic worth, but because I regard it as the stepping-stone to my present greatest possession—the true friendship of Ada Caldara.

CARMICHAEL'S CHRISTMAS
SPIRIT

CARMICHAEL'S CHRISTMAS
SPIRIT

THE bachelor apartments of Henry Carmichael had long been mildly celebrated among the many young women who counted themselves his friends. It was not the unusual luxury of the rooms, although there was quite enough of that, too, even for a young man with a carefully invested fortune and no real responsibilities; but Carmichael had in many ways strongly impressed upon the place his own personality. During his thirty years of life he had travelled far and in many different directions, and had met many people. Inherited wealth and position, to which he had added geography, had supplied him with numberless chance acquaintances and a few friends, and long since he had adopted the excellent practice of never keeping a letter or destroying a photograph.

Thus the story of his life—it so pleased his young women friends to believe—was somewhere to be found carefully framed, and more or less carefully autographed, about the little study wherein he read the morning papers and wrote and accepted invitations to dinner. The only difficulty was to find *the* photograph among the many, and the variety of the subjects and their constant kaleidoscopic change from ostentatious conspicuousness to almost total eclipse added no little zest to the game. The gallery of feminine beauty covered the walls, interfered with the face of the clock on the mantel over the fireplace, cramped his writing-desk, and suffocated the big centre table.

There were heavily framed photographs that looked like mezzotints, of women in flowered brocades, women who ruled modern society in New York and London and Paris; little photographs of young girls in simple dinner dresses or short duck skirts and sailor hats, who some day would rule, too, in their mothers' places; pictures of women of the Paris stage and the café concerts, signed with the most sincere expressions of regard and undying affection; little and big photographs of every kind of the present day Broadway favorites, from skittish

soubrettes and smiling ingénues to hollow-eyed leading women and ponderous dramatic sopranos from
the Metropolitan Opera House. Mixed with this in-
congruous collection was here and there a picture of
a handsome Englishwoman, who from her signature
of one name and her coronet could easily be detected
as a person of title; and the gallery even boasted of
one woman who would some day, if she lived long
enough, wear a real crown.

On this particular Christmas eve Carmichael came
into his study and smilingly glanced about at the
array of photographic friends, and then, assuming a
more serious aspect, went into the dining-room and
looked over the carefully arranged table. His knowing
eye travelled quickly over the snow-white damask,
the thin tall glasses with their tapering stems, the
heavy silver, and the great bunch of American
beauties rising above a massive loving cup, which he
himself had won at golf. With a smile of content the
young man returned once more to the study, lit a
cigarette, and waited.

He did not have long to wait; for as the clock
chimed eight Miss Rita Maynard was shown in, and

Carmichael greeted her with the effusion of a very old and admiring friend.

"Am I the very first?" she asked.

Carmichael paid no heed to her question; but took one of her hands in each of his, and, spreading them apart, looked with undisguised admiration at the broad clear brow, the crisp curling hair, the slanting eyes, the pink cheeks with their wonderful contour, the full rounded throat, and the ivory shoulders.

"Rita, you know," he said at last, dropping her hands, "it isn't right to look like that. I saw you the other night some place, and thought then that you had hung up an entirely new record for beauty; but —really, you know, if I looked in my glass and saw something like that I should feel just as much pleased as if I had written a great novel or composed a national anthem."

"How about the dress-maker?" and Miss Maynard glanced with a smile of pride down at the straight filmy white dress.

"Beautiful!" he said. "And of course that all helps; but really you oughtn't to go to a bachelor apartment looking like that; it's not safe."

Miss Maynard crossed over to the fireplace and, resting both hands on the mantel shelf, looked at the long row of photographs.

"I'm not afraid," she said. "Indeed, Harry, I don't know any place where one feels so well chaperoned as here—dowagers and duchesses all about one, and simple innocent little girls who ought to be in short frocks instead of ball dresses; and then all these stage ladies who would fairly battle for you if you looked at another woman—that is, if you are willing to believe half they write on their photographs. What became of the girl you used to have here in front of the clock? She was a very impressive blonde as I remember her; looked like a young matron. The present one seems to have rather dark hair and an angel-child smirk. Who is she?"

Carmichael went over to the fireplace and took up the photograph and, looking at it carefully, drew his lips in to a straight line. "That's a very nice girl," he said. "The features of the blonde matron got harder and harder every day. I don't know whether it was leaning against those jangling chimes, or just married life; but I had to sky her." He waved his hand in the direction of the panel over the doorway. "There she is, between Mettie Carlisle, the lady in the bathing suit, and Lady Margaret Donald, the British personage with her hair in a mop. And she'll stay there too. Anybody that has to be hung with a step-ladder has reached her final niche in my gallery. She never can be a head-liner again."

"What an awful fate!" Miss Maynard sighed. "It was very good of you to ask us to-night. Who are 'us'?"

"Well, there are the Jim Hoaglands, and the Arthur Lowrys, and Ledyard and his wife, and the Henrys, and you and I—ten of us."

"My!" said Miss Maynard, "but that crowd does make one feel terribly unmarried! Every time I look about the table I shall feel that I've shirked my responsibilities."

"Not at all; I asked them on purpose. They're all married, and naturally all play bridge. After dinner I'm going to have two tables in the library, and you and I can come out here and talk it over."

"The dinner?" she asked, raising her eyebrows.

"Rita," he said, "if you look like that I'm likely to talk or rave about anything!"

"Even me, Harry?"

"Even you, Rita, even you."

And then the other guests began to arrive, and for the time being Carmichael saw little of Miss Maynard.

"This dinner," said Carmichael when they were all seated at table, "is the result of a purely selfish idea of mine to bring a little of what is called the Christmas spirit into a poor bachelor's apartment. I can't call it a home because any bachelor apartment is a disgrace to the name. I suppose you good married women would have preferred a few unattached young men to chat with you, and you old men would have rather liked to sit between very foolish young girls; but I wanted only old friends and the kind who might leave a little of the aroma of home about the place after you had gone back to your Christmas trees. Rita's presence needs no excuse. She is the only *jeune fille* here; first, because she is my oldest friend, for we played together as children, and second, because she doesn't play bridge now."

"Is this a speech?" asked Hoagland. "Because if it is I should think this would be the psychological moment to drink somebody's health—Miss Maynard's preferred by all means."

"All right," said Carmichael; "but before I conclude my rhetoric I want to warn you that you bridge players had better fix your points now, because while the dinner is to be short it will be rather rich and conducive to large stakes."

After this Carmichael gave way to the others, and the dinner passed on as happily as small, well-appointed dinners among friends are apt to do. Being but a small party, the conversation was general; so that every story, even every new and old joke, had its listeners, and before the end every one had drunk jokingly to the good health of every one else; that is, except in the case of the toast to Carmichael. This was proposed by Rita Maynard, and perhaps it was on account of the wonderful beauty of the girl, as she stood with her uplifted glass, or perhaps it was that in her voice and in her manner there was a certain note of sincerity; but whatever it was, the toast was quite different from the others.

"I propose," she had said, with a certain hesitation in her words, "that we drink to the good health and happiness of our host, and also to his hope that he may find a little of the Christmas spirit to-night after we have gone. For all the kindly things he has done during his lifetime, I think he deserves it more than any one I know."

True to the host's word, the dinner was a short one, and it was not much later than nine when, the tables having been set for bridge, the game was well under way, and Miss Maynard and Carmichael had returned to the little study.

"Did you ever see the view from these windows on a winter night like this?" Carmichael asked, as he pulled back the curtains. The girl crossed the room to his side, and for some moments they stood at the high French windows silently looking out on the park, a great stretch of newly fallen snow and the trees sheathed in ice, and every twig and branch glistening in the white glare of the electric lights.

"No," she said, "I don't think I ever have. You know this is the first time I have been here this year.

It's quite wonderful, isn't it? Harry, we don't see nearly enough of each other in winter."

"I know. It really seems as if we could get together only in summer, doesn't it? But I think that is usually the way with one's real friends. That was a nice little speech you made, Rita, very nice." And he dropped his hand to his side and gave hers a gentle pressure. "I suppose," he continued, "if you really wanted to, you could get the true Christmas spirit out there in the snow? Even now there may be some poor devil freezing in the park yonder, and you wouldn't have to look very far through the tenements over on the West Side to get a chance to make a hit as Santa Claus, would you?"

Miss Maynard walked over to the fire and settled back in a deep easy chair, with the tips of her satin slippers resting on the fender. "Is that your idea of the Christmas spirit?" she asked.

Carmichael still stood looking out at the snow and beating a slow tattoo on the window pane with his knuckles. "Oh, I don't know just what I do mean. I suppose the real significance of the day has al' gone, so far as I am concerned; but it's left a sort of general desire to want to do something for somebody for no particular reason." The young man came over and sat on a low stool at the girl's feet, with his back to the fire.

"It's just one of those bugaboos that all we bachelors fall heir to. For some reason I never can separate the idea of home and Christmas. You can hang up all the red-ribboned wreaths you choose, and you can dress your married friends' trees for your married friends' children, and you can eat your married friends' Christmas dinners; but it isn't really Christmas, because it isn't really home."

Miss Maynard glanced about the room. "Some people would call this a pretty good home; and you seem to have plenty of friends," she added, nodding her head at the long row of photographs on the shelf over the fireplace.

"Those photographs? They're a bluff. You know what I mean, Rita."

"Of course I know what you mean, and I'm glad of it. Sometimes, Harry, I'm only afraid you won't feel that way about things. I know there are a lot of foolish women who make a fuss over you, and I fear sometimes you can't stand it and that it will make you different. Are all these photographs bluffs?"

Carmichael nodded. "Pretty much. You know how it is. Men affect women so differently. There are some men, generally very fine citizens, whom women fly from, and there are others they want to fly with, and still others they want to give their photographs to and have to tea when their husbands are downtown. I'm in the last class. Then, I suppose, they have heard of my gallery of international beauties, and want to be represented."

From the table at her side Miss Maynard picked up a large photograph of herself in a silver frame and looked at it quite impersonally. "A bluff?" she asked, holding it up so that Carmichael could see it.

"No," he said, "that is the only picture that I insist must never be moved. It's a permanent quantity—always been in the same place for years."

"Always in the same place for years?" the girl repeated slowly. "Who changes the others, then, with so much taste, and creates all this mystery in the breasts of your young women friends?"

"My man does all that," Carmichael answered

promptly, "and it's one of his most cherished perquisites. It doesn't cost me anything, and it gives him a great deal of pleasure. He's terribly fickle, though —he features two or three a week some weeks. And what he sees in some of them I cannot understand, and yet it seems a little familiar for me to ask him. There was a hand-painted photograph of a Hungarian dancer that he was crazy about. He set her up against my ink-well first, and when I threw her into the waste-paper basket he fished her out and leaned her against the lamp on the table there. It lit her up like a spotlight. I hid her behind books and in closets and in every out-of-the-way corner in the place; but the next day there she would be with her tinted beauty presiding over the dining-room or the bath-room or any old place, till I had to cremate her in the grate."

"It's little wonder then," said Miss Maynard, "that no one has ever been able to find the real one."

Carmichael smiled and clasped his hands about his knees. "Ah!" he repeated, "the real one, eh?"

The girl sat up straight in her chair, and in imitation of her host clasped her hands about her knees and then looked him fairly in the eyes. "Yes, please

311

tell me, Harry; I'm such an old friend. Which is *the* one?"

Carmichael smiled up at the girl, and then slowly pulled himself to his feet. "You don't mind if I smoke, do you?"

Miss Maynard shook her head, and the young man crossed the room to find a cigar, and then returned to his place at the fire. He took a match-box from his pocket, and as he slowly lit his cigar the red light from the hearth fell full on his face.

"After all, Rita," he said, "what's the use?"

The girl impulsively put out her hand and laid it on his arm. "Why, Harry," she whispered, "I'm so sorry! I didn't understand. You know we've seen so little of each other lately. I thought they were all— you know—just bluffs." The girl tossed her head toward the pictures over the fireplace.

"Well," he said, "so they are; *the* one is the only one that isn't here. Don't you believe, Rita, that every author knows one story that he never writes, and every painter one picture that he would rather starve than put on canvas? I do.

"But she used to be here," he went on. "There

was a little picture of her on the table over there and another on the top of the desk, and one on the mantel, and there was a big one on the piano. Wherever you looked you could see her. She was everywhere; at least, so it seemed to me. And there was another one of her on my bureau. She looked particularly bright in that one, and sort of piquant and very cheery, and every morning when I got up I used to say good-morning to her."

Miss Maynard leaned forward, resting her elbows on her knees and holding her chin between the palms of her hands. "You knew her very well," she asked, "and for a long time?"

Carmichael nodded. "Yes, for quite a long time—too long, I suppose."

"What—what was she like, Harry? Do you mind?"

Carmichael stared at the fire and shook his head. "No, of course I don't mind," he said; "that is, to you. I like to talk about her."

For some moments he hesitated, and then went on again. "It's hard, in a way, because it's so difficult to give one an idea of personality, and that's about

313

all that really counts, isn't it? She was very pretty too, in a way—her expression was always changing; it seemed as if it reflected every shade of every thought and idea she had, and she certainly had wonderful thoughts and ideas. I think she had the clearest, cleanest grasp of things and the broadest and most sane philosophy of life of any woman or man I have ever known. I suppose it was because she had had rather a hard time of it, and experience had taught her much that many girls never know. She had what the artist folk call temperament, too, and with her intelligence she ought to have made the greatest actress of our day."

"She was on the stage?" Miss Maynard asked.

"Yes, still is."

"Isn't she clever—I mean on the stage?"

Carmichael shook his head. "No, and never will be, I imagine. With all her intelligence and good looks, she lacks the one essential thing—the trick the actors call 'getting it over the footlights.'"

"Then why——"

"Why," interrupted Carmichael—"why? Oh, just because she is independent and doesn't want to admit failure. I don't think the stage meant anything to her but her rent and board; but she liked to pay for those herself, and I think the success of other women, with only half her talents, annoyed her and hurt her pride, and she had a great deal of that."

For some moments there was silence, while Carmichael twisted his cigar slowly between his lips and the girl still sat looking into the fire. It was she who broke the silence.

"Who were her friends?"

"I don't know. I don't know that she had any real friends. The first time I met her was at a sort of Bohemian supper, and I couldn't understand exactly why she was there at all. She worried me a good deal for a time; that is, until I got to know her. I thought at first that she must be ignorant of their moral point of view, because I knew from everything about her that she couldn't possibly share it. And then afterward I talked to her about it, and her knowledge was just as much greater than mine as her charity was. Why, Rita, she saw people just as we would see things through that magnifying glass over there on the table. For a long time after that she used to come here in

THE STAGE DOOR

the afternoon and sit at the tea-table and drink tea, and I would drink Scotch and smoke and listen to her. It was wonderful how she accepted her share of life always with a smile on her lips."

"Still," said the girl, "her share of life was more or less what she made it. After all, her lot might have been different; that is, if I understand you—I mean how much you cared."

"Yes, it might have been different," Carmichael said; "but she chose her failure on the stage and the hall bedroom and the one dress and the one hat. I tell you, Rita, the hall bedroom and the one dress and the one hat have had almost as much effect on some girls' lives in this town as mothers' prayers. What do you think?"

For answer Miss Maynard sat back in the deep chair and, looking at Carmichael, slowly shook her head. "I think," she said, "there must have been some other reason. Admitting that she had the highest motives in the world, it is difficult to understand why she should have chosen the hall bedroom instead of all this." The girl glanced about the room and then back at Carmichael. "Of course, Harry, if you were an ogre, it would have been different; but you are not an ogre. In fact, I understand all mothers and most daughters call you eligible. It really seems as if she might have brought herself to care a little."

"Perhaps," said Carmichael, slowly weighing his words, "perhaps she cared too much. She had an absurd idea of the world that you, for instance, belong to; probably because she knew so little of it. I think you represented to her everything that a woman ought to be—certainly the type of woman I ought to marry."

"I?"

"Yes, you. I had talked to her a lot about you, and——"

"And the one photograph," Miss Maynard interrupted, "that was never moved?"

Carmichael nodded. "I suppose so. She said that her visits here were nothing but a bundle of faded letters tied with a ribbon and hid away in the bureau drawer at the actors' boarding-house—the kind of letters that a woman marks 'Burn without opening,' and only reads when her husband is downtown and she is discouraged and wants to bring on a good cry."

"And what was the end of all this? There's always an end."

"The end was that she was very ill, and I did everything that a man who has a certain amount of brains and a good deal of money could do for a woman. The fact that she was sick made it possible, where it wasn't possible before."

"And then?" the girl asked.

"And then I found out, just as every man finds out when a woman he cares for is really ill: it's the only perfectly sure test I know. And when she was quite well and at work again, and her pride had come back, I asked her to tea, and after tea, I told her my discovery. It was a very important one to me; but not to her, it seemed. Then I collected all her photographs, and we sat here just as you and I are sitting here to-night, and one by one I tore the photographs in two and put them in the fire and they burned up. I told her that I was a strong man, and liked a fight; but I knew when I was beaten: that it was a case of marrying me, or saying good-by. That evening I went out to my cottage at Rye, where I made the caretaker cook for a friend and me for two days. For those two days I did exactly what I had always read about men doing in novels and what I had seen them do on the stage. I tramped up and down and talked and raved about her to the man whom I had brought along for the purpose, and he was just as sympathetic as I knew he was going to be. At the end of two days I had exhausted myself and my friend, and I came back here to the blank spaces where her photographs used to be and to the empty wicker chair where she used to sit.

"That is all a year ago, and since those two days until to-night I have never spoken to any one about her; but the blank spaces are still blank spaces, although they have been filled with many faces; and the spirit of home which she brought here in those days is just as lacking to me as if the rooms were stripped and the packing boxes were standing in the hallway."

"And you have never seen her since?"

"Yes. Several times on the stage, and once, just the other day, I met her in the street."

"Did you speak to her?"

"No; but I wanted to take her in my arms and carry her away—anywhere. There was such a tired

319

look in her eyes, and her face was so peaked, and she seemed so terribly worn and poor."

"And you didn't speak to her?"

"No; she would have preferred it that way. I know her so well, Rita."

"Perhaps—one never knows. Women have been known to change."

Carmichael looked up and smilingly shook his head. "Not this woman," he said.

"Is she playing here now?" Miss Maynard asked. "I suppose it's absurdly curious of me; but I should like to see her after all that you have told me."

"Yes, she's playing down the street at the Majestic. Her name is Alice Yorke, and she plays the part of a younger sister, and her performance is just as bad as the play. I've seen it a dozen times or more, and I ought to know. It's terrible."

Miss Maynard smiled cheerfully. "Come on, Harry. I hear the others coming, and I must be going home; it's nearly eleven o'clock now. Are you going to the club or any place that I can drop you?"

"No, thank you, Rita," he said. "I think I'll read a bit and go to bed."

They were joined a moment later by the bridge players, who impressively thanked Carmichael for his true hospitality in leaving them so uninterruptedly alone to their game. And then they told him individually and in chorus how much they had enjoyed the dinner, and every one bade every one else good-night and exchanged the best of wishes for a merry Christmas.

For just a moment after the others had left the room Rita Maynard lingered while Carmichael arranged her cloak for her.

"Thank you so much, Harry!" she whispered. "It was such a good friendly talk. Don't think too long of the blank spaces. Good-night and good luck."

Five minutes later Miss Maynard's automobile drew up at the stage door of the Majestic Theatre, and the door-keeper was so overcome by the radiant beauty of the young woman and the richness of her mantle that for once he forgot to be churlish and promptly led her to the deserted stage.

The performance had been over for some little time; but the door-keeper was quite sure that Miss Yorke was still in her dressing-room. In any case he would make sure, and so he climbed the spiral staircase which led to the dressing-rooms and told Miss Yorke that the most beautiful "society" lady he had ever seen was waiting for her with an automobile.

The two women met on the dimly lit stage, and, perhaps it was from the unusual surroundings, or for one reason or another, it was only the visitor who showed any signs of embarrassment.

"I'm Miss Maynard," she began, "and my only excuse for coming to see you to-night is that I am a very old friend of a friend of yours—Harry Carmichael."

Miss Yorke smiled brightly and put out her hand. "I am very glad to meet you," she said. "Mr. Carmichael is, or was, a great friend of mine."

For a moment the actress waited, while Miss Maynard mentally groped about for the words with which to explain her mission. The poise of the girl, and something in the ease of her manner and the frankness with which she met her glance, was a little confusing.

"Have you anything to do—now, I mean?" Miss Maynard asked.

Miss Yorke shook her head. "Nothing," she said.

"Well, if you don't think it too great an impertinence, I'm going to ask you if you won't take a little drive with me through the park. I want to say something to you so much, and I could say it so much better to you there than here."

"I'd love to go," Miss Yorke said, and smilingly glanced about at the heavy set-pieces, the rows of flat scenes piled up against rough brick walls, and the watch light with its single gas flame burning dimly in the centre of the stage. "I'm afraid it is rather confusing to you here," she added. "Shall we go?"

Just what was said between the two girls in Miss Maynard's automobile that night as they raced over the snow-covered roads of the deserted park has never been, and in all probability never will be, known. And the reason for this no doubt is that although until that night they had been strangers, each girl must have told the other something that heretofore she had kept in her own heart and had never told to any one. But, be that as it may, at least the result of that talk is now well known.

At the hour when Santa Claus was at his busiest,

filling stockings with candy and toys and hanging gold stars and little pink cupids on Christmas trees all over the big city, Rita Maynard's automobile stopped once more that night at the home of Henry Carmichael. The two girls went up to the floor of his apartment together, and when Carmichael himself came to the door in answer to their ring he found them standing together, with Rita Maynard's arm about the shoulders of her new friend.

For just a moment Carmichael stood in the doorway a little dazed; and then he understood, and held out his arms to her.

"Harry," Miss Maynard said, "I've brought you a little of the Christmas spirit you were talking about." And then she gently urged Alice Yorke toward the doorway. "I'll wait for you in the car," she added; "don't be long."

When Rita Maynard had left Miss Yorke at the actors' boarding-house on the West Side, and her work was done, and well done, she started for her own home. Her cloak drawn tightly about her throat and shoulders, her arms folded, her head resting against the cushions, the girl with wide-open eyes stared at the design of the brocade with which the top of the automobile was lined.

It was just midnight when she reached her destination, and the bells were ringing out the news which has meant so many things to so many people for so many years. She got out of the automobile, and had almost reached the steps of her home, when the clamor of the bells seemed to bring her back to herself and her surroundings, and she turned toward the chauffeur.

"Good-night, Donald," she said, "and a Merry Christmas to you."

The chauffeur smiled broadly, nodded, and touched his cap. "Thank you, miss," he said; "and a Merry Christmas to you too."

For a moment the girl hesitated while the two words of thanks which she would have spoken died in her throat, and with uncertain steps and misty eyes she went slowly on up the steps of her home.

THE ROAD TO GLORY

THE ROAD TO GLORY

'COME in!" said the Junior Partner.

The door to the private office opened, and a young girl stood silhouetted against the glare of yellow light of the big room outside.

"Did you wish to see me, Mr. Grey?" the girl asked.

The Junior Partner glanced up from the mass of papers lying on his desk. "No, Miss Lorelle; I wanted Miss Agnew."

"I'm afraid she's gone home; it's after six o'clock."

"Of course, of course, I quite forgot," Grey said. "I wanted her to take a letter for me. You are not a stenographer, are you?"

She smiled and shook her head. "I'm afraid not. Could I write it in long hand?"

The Junior Partner turned to his papers. "No, thank you," he said. "I suppose every one has gone?"

"Yes, every one." The girl closed the door softly and returned to her desk.

The Junior Partner signed the first few letters of the many that lay before him, and then pushed the remainder petulantly away from him. He swung slowly about on his swivel chair and looked with unseeing eyes at the walls of the little room. It was an unusually attractive room for an office. Above the walnut wainscoting there hung some fine old portraits of the founders of the firm, and the rest of the room fairly lived up to the dignity of the old gentlemen in the very high collars and the ruffled shirt fronts. The dark-green curtains, which were drawn, were of heavy brocade, and the deep leather chairs and sofa were of substantial build and almost luxurious in their comfort. The light from a coal grate glowed on andirons and a fender of highly polished brass, and beyond threw flickering shadows across a rug of much softness and great warmth of color. The fire-light, and the desk lamp of one lonely shaded globe, made but a feeble effort toward brightening the dull surroundings.

The Junior Partner swung clear around on his

chair, touched an electric bell on the desk for the second time that evening, and then, with sudden dexterity, took his stand in front of the fireplace. "Come in, Miss Lorelle!" he called.

The young girl came in and waited in the centre of the room, standing fairly in the light of the fire. The Junior Partner glanced at the black dress, closely fitted to the tall, lithe figure; at the white paper cuff pinned on her writing arm; and at the lace collar about the full white throat. Without meeting her eyes, he motioned to one of two large arm-chairs that stood on each side of the hearth. "Won't you sit down?" he said.

The girl inclined her head and moved with a grace of great charm until she found herself in front of the chair. Then she suddenly seemed to become conscious of the fact that to sit about a fire with a member of the firm of which she was a humble employee was an entirely new and rather humorous sensation. She cast one glance of protest at the Junior Partner, and then, clumsily enough, sat down, hunched up on the edge of the big arm-chair.

The Junior Partner sat far back in his chair

331

opposite her, crossed his legs, and for a few moments gazed reflectively into the fireplace. He was accounted a very clever business man; but he was also a very young man, and so he approached a new situation with a manner which was always intentionally deliberate and often unconvincing.

"Miss Lorelle," he said slowly, "I think I had the pleasure of seeing you the other night in the palace scene of 'The King's Fool.' Am I right?"

The girl did not look up, but clasped her hands slowly about her right knee, and interlaced the fingers tightly together. "Yes," she said. "I wondered at the time if you had recognized me." For a few moments she groped about for something more to say, while the young man gazed steadfastly at the burning coals. "Did you like the play, Mr. Grey?" she asked at last.

"I liked you," Grey said.

Miss Lorelle smiled and glanced at him from the corner of her eye. "I don't quite understand—I only walk on in that one scene. An extra girl could hardly impress one, I should think, very much one way or the other."

"Not at all," said the Junior Partner. "It was because you stood out so easily from the rest and with so little opportunity, that I liked you. And then besides you had a few lines which I thought you read uncommonly well."

"That's right, I did have lines that night. They don't really belong to me, but the girl who usually has them was away."

Once more the conversation flagged even more ominously than before. This time it was the man who broke the silence. "Did you ever seriously consider going on the stage?"

The girl unclasped her hands and slid back into the depths of the big leather chair. The glow from the coals fell full on the wavy mass of hair brushed back clear from the broad white forehead, on the oval face, on the slanting eyes, the delicately pencilled eyebrows, the heavy lashes, and the finely cut nose and chin. A faint flush rose above the swelling throat and spread over the cheeks and temples. "Yes, sometimes I have thought I should like to go on the stage," she said. "I mean regularly. Why?"

"You have never been on the stage—regularly?"

She put one hand over her eyes, as if to shut out the firelight. Grey sat forward and, resting his elbows on his knees, held his chin tightly between the palms of his hands. It was some moments before the girl spoke. When she did her voice sounded metallic and tired.

"Yes," she said at last. "I was on the stage once. When I first came to New York I went to a dramatic school, more for amusement than anything else. Then one day my uncle, who had always supported me, told me that he had lost a lot of money, and the remittances must stop, and that I must go back to the little town where he lived, or look out for myself. Well, I would rather have died than go back, and so I got an engagement with a very bad company. It was a road company—we never played near New York. We went to pieces in Duluth, and had to beat and beg our way back. It was not a nice experience."

"And then?" asked the Junior Partner.

"Then? Oh, then I got letters from my uncle, who still had some business connections in New York and I worked in two or three offices, and—and finally

I came here. I didn't tell Mr. Wiley anything about my theatrical experience when he engaged me."

"Why?" interrupted Grey.

"Why? You know the reputation of this office— every girl that comes here is supposed to vouch for both her great-grandmothers. To get in here is supposed to be a sort of a decoration in my world."

"But you are not happy here. Whenever I see you at your desk you always seem to be dreaming about something. Why, even to-night you see how late you are with your work; and you know it is the same nearly every night, don't you?"

She took her hand from before her face and nodded gravely into the grave eyes of the young man. "Yes," she said, "I know. It does seem as if I were always late."

"You'll pardon me, Miss Lorelle," Grey went on; "but it seems to me that your temperament is essentially suited to the life of an actress, and not to your present work. Your voice, your face, your figure, are all assets, if you will allow me to say so, which I think are lost in an office such as this. You have altogether too much imagination—a clerk should be a machine. I am going to ask you a plain question. Why remain a bad clerk at fifteen dollars a week, when you might be a good actress at many times that sum? This life is well enough for these other girls here; but not for you—not for you."

The girl slowly clasped her hands behind her head and looked wide eyed at the Junior Partner. "I suppose it all means," she whispered, "that I must go— that this is really a polite way of telling me that you don't want me any longer."

The young man rose and for a moment stood with his back to her, resting his hands on the mantel shelf over the fire. He was a very young man. "Believe me, Miss Lorelle," he said, turning to her again. "I am speaking for your best interests as well as our own. I'm sure I could get you an engagement. I know at least one manager who would be only too glad to oblige me. I want to be fair to you, Miss Lorelle; indeed I do. It has always been a tradition of this firm to treat its people with every consideration—with every kindness that was possible."

For a brief moment she pressed her hand slowly against her eyes, and then took it quickly away again, and slid out of the deep chair. "Oh, I know," she said, standing. "You are kind—very kind to your people—you even mean to be kind to me. Good-night."

The Junior Partner held out his hand. "You won't be leaving us for some days, I hope."

Miss Lorelle brushed the tips of her fingers across his open palm.

"Yes, to-night. Miss Crawford can do my work. I'll explain everything to her in a letter. I wouldn't care to see the girls again."

"And you won't let me write to this manager?"

The girl had regained her habitual poise, and, turning at the doorway, smiled back at him, and shook her head. "I'm afraid you're a little too young and too good looking and much too rich to start a girl on the stage—that is, for the girl's good. Good-night—and good-by to you, Mr. Grey."

The door closed sharply behind her, and the Junior Partner was left alone to finish his letters. Half an hour later when he passed through the big office room he saw her still working. He turned and gravely bowed in her direction; but the only answer was the scratching of the girl's pen over the unbalanced journal.

The morning after the leave taking of Miss Lorelle six of the seven young women who worked in the large room arrived promptly at nine o'clock, and were proceeding with much deliberation to remove their hats and wraps, when they were suddenly startled by a cry of consternation from the direction of Miss Crawford's desk. The girls promptly gathered about their fellow-clerk and gazed anxiously on the letter which she held in her hand, and which without doubt had been the cause of the excitement. With much emphasis Miss Crawford read the document aloud to her fellow-workers. It was a very simple letter, saying good-by to six young women whom during working hours Miss Lorelle had known rather intimately, and of whom in her own way she was very fond. When the signature of the letter had been read with proper emphasis, the five young women who had been standing about Miss Crawford's desk gazed at each other with wide-eyed wonder. The idea of an employee leaving the firm of

Wiley, Grey & Co. overnight was without prece-
dent, and almost criminal in its suddenness.

Anna Wilson, a black-eyed girl in short dresses,
who was really a girl office boy, and much the
youngest of the group, made slight effort to control
her feelings, and, burying her head in her arms on
Miss Crawford's desk, burst into violent weeping.
It was the first break she had ever experienced in
an official family, and besides Miss Lorelle had
always treated her with great kindness and just as
if she were not a very young girl but a woman like
the rest of them. Perhaps it was shock or perhaps
it was that the other girl clerks shared the feeling of
Miss Wilson, weeping on the desk, and had a better
control over the lumps that were rising and falling
in their throats; but in any case there were many
moments of silence that followed the reading of the
letter. Each of these girls knew that Miss Lorelle
was not a good clerk, each of them knew also that
she individually had helped her constantly with
her work, and had done her best to shield her de-
ficiencies from the ever-watchful eyes of the Junior Partner. And yet at that moment they would

have given up many hours of their own time to have seen her back at her old desk. Perhaps it was the thoughtfulness of the girl who had left them that inspired these thoughts, or perhaps it was her flower-like beauty, or perhaps it was the unspoken thought that she was just a little different from themselves—of a slightly different mould and of just a trifle finer clay.

Be that as it may, any further discussion of the situation was rendered impossible by the appearance of the Junior Partner. For a moment he stopped at the desk of Miss Crawford and arranged for a fair division of Miss Lorelle's work until her successor should have been selected. With these slight changes, the work of the office, at least outwardly, continued on its even way.

It is probable that had Miss Lorelle returned to the daily grind of desk work in another quarter of the city, or had she pursued some equally unostentatious calling, the record of her recent business life would have fast faded into a pleasant memory. But Miss Lorelle, after some consideration, returned to the stage, not so much on account of the advice of her late employer, as because it seemed to be the course that offered the least resistance. With her knowledge of the possibilities of the profession, she turned to the agencies, and frequented them with such persistency that in little more than a week she was on her way to Denver to fill a minor position in a summer stock company. For two months she played twice a day and rehearsed and the best part of the remainder of each twenty-four hours worked on her wardrobe. It was very hard work, but at least it taught her ease and the rudiments of acting.

Late in August, when a Chicago manager "discovered" her, he found her a little pale and tired— quite tired enough to abandon any immediate hope she may have had of becoming a dramatic star. He wanted her for a small part in a musical comedy— that is, if she could sing and dance—and as she could do a little of both, she was promptly engaged. In a few weeks she was at work again; but after her experience with the stock company it seemed more like play. With her one song, which happened to be a good song, she attained a certain amount of success.

But it was, after all, her beauty that scored and that gave her a probably unwarranted local reputation. Paragraphs occasionally appeared about her in the Chicago newspapers, and in her really gorgeous stage dresses and her imitation pearls she was constantly in demand for "art studies" by the local photographers. In time these pictures appeared in the magazines, and were usually accompanied by rather startling tales of the past and present of this new and extremely beautiful addition to the American stage. She had confidingly placed herself in the hands of her press agent and he had supplied her lavishly with an imaginary private electric brougham, a French touring car, and jewels that would make a rajah fairly wince with envy.

During the winter months these pictures and the wonder tales of the new spendthrift beauty reached New York and eventually found their way into the big room of Wiley, Grey & Co., where they were welcomed with sighs of delight and without an iota of doubt as to their absolute truthfulness. Notwithstanding the somewhat décolleté appearance of Miss Lorelle in the photographic studies, she became at once the patron saint of the office where she had so recently been a humble employé. Every desk contained one or more of her pictures, and every morsel of news as to her last escapade was read aloud to wide-eyed wonderment. Her past life in the big room was gone over with wonderful minuteness, and her every simple kindness was developed into a deed of splendid heroism. And through all this spirit of loyalty and admiration there was no word nor thought of envy. One of their own had one night passed out of their workaday, monotonous life and had suddenly appeared as a brilliant light in a world of which these girls could only read and of which they could really know but little. In the natural course of events it was quite sure that some day she must return to New York, and the seven young women waited patiently for the day.

This day came early in June. It was the first of the summer musical productions, and the New York first-nighters awaited the event with no unusual display of interest. Miss Lorelle had been featured in the newspapers to the exact limit that the woman star and the comedian would permit, and it must be said that the audience, when it saw her, liked this new girl from the West. They liked her almost perfect beauty, and they liked the way she moved about the stage, and a certain conviction with which she read her lines, and, above all else, the unusual intelligence which she used in singing her one song. It was very far from an ovation; but her reception was out of all proportion to the part she played, and the critics, who like the unusual, said as much in their reviews the morning following. With one accord they dismissed the light voice with a few words, and stopped to praise at some length the beauty and the resources of this young girl who had found flowers where the authors had planted only weeds.

It is probable that at no one place in New York were these notices so eagerly read, or so much discussed, as in the big room of Wiley, Grey & Co. The seven girls laughed and rejoiced over them, perhaps even cried a little over them, and mentally agreed never to buy one paper again because it fell far below the others in praising their favorite. Individually they had each sent her a telegram, and collectively they were represented by a large bunch of roses, the cost of which was out of all proportion to their weekly salaries. Exactly how she was to acknowledge these tokens of regard was a matter of no little moment, and was as frequently and vivaciously discussed the day following the début as were the notices in the morning newspapers. Some believed that she would return their thoughtfulness in kind, telegram for telegram and flower for flower, while others hoped for nothing more than one polite note of thanks that would cover all cases.

The matter was decided late in the afternoon, when Miss Lorelle herself appeared in the doorway of the big room. For a brief moment the seven young women sat staring open-eyed at this wonderful vision of loveliness laughing and walking toward them with outstretched hands, and then, wholly forgetting that the lady in the salmon-pink cloth dress was their patron saint, they ran to her and threw their arms about her and remembered only that she was their old friend Maggie Lorelle. To a chorus of many questions and hysterical laughter she was half dragged, half carried, to the nearest desk, where they put her down in a chair, and then all gathered about, as closely as they conveniently could. Some sat on the desk, and others sat on the floor, and still others had to content themselves with an outer fringe of chairs. For a few moments there was silence, while Miss Lorelle beamed joyously at the seven young women, and the eyes of the seven young women strayed from the close-fitting salmon-pink coat to the creaseless skirt, the patent leather ties, the black silk stockings, the glistening white kid gloves, and the black picture hat with the great bow of pink velvet.

Miss Cregar, who was usually regarded as the dean of the clerks, was the first to break these moments of silent adulation. "Maggie," she said, "I want you to know Miss Bowles—she's the girl that took your place when you left."

A young girl with very red cheeks sitting on the floor blushed violently, although in the confusion she had embraced Miss Lorelle as enthusiastically as the others.

Miss Lorelle smiled cheerfully and took the girl's outstretched hand in both of hers. "I have to thank you for a telegram, and for your share in the roses. That was the best part of last night, girls—the tele-

grams and your flowers." There was a very slight
quaver in the voice of the speaker. "You see, it
showed me how you all remembered me, and that
you had probably been interested in what I was
doing."

"Oh, we followed you all right," said Anna Wilson
from her perch on the top of the desk. "We saw all
your pictures in the papers and the magazines, and
we read all they said about you, and the automobiles
and the diamonds you got. Did you come down here
in your automobile?"

Miss Lorelle looked up suddenly into the eyes of
the speaker and then into those of the little group
gathered about her. The stories of the diamonds and
the automobiles had been regarded so differently by
different people.

"No," said the actress, smiling again, "I didn't
come in my automobile, because, you see, I haven't
got one."

"Haven't got one!" they echoed in chorus.

"Why, I saw a picture of you," Miss Wilson
argued, "and you were stepping into your private
electric hansom with two men on the box. It was in

front of a grand house with a garden as big as a public park."

"No, I haven't got a single automobile, nor even one little diamond."

Keen disappointment was clearly written on the faces about her.

"You see, all those stories were published just to advertise the show I was with."

"And the beautiful flat in Chicago?" asked Miss Wilson.

Miss Lorelle shook her head, and fairly laughed aloud. "Just a dream of the press agent. When he wrote that story, I was living in a boarding-house, trying to save enough money to buy a few good clothes and some imitation pearls."

"And the man that wrote that knew it all the time?" asked a dismayed voice from the fringe of chairs.

"All the time," said Miss Lorelle.

"And you have to ride all rigged up like a horse in the street cars and the 'L'?" Miss Wilson asked almost tearfully.

"Well, not always, Anna, dear, because, you see,

348

I'm not very often rigged up like a horse. It's only when I make a formal call like this that I wear my good clothes. Besides——"

"I saw a picture of you," interrupted Miss Wilson, "in a sable coat that dragged on the ground. Don't tell us you don't own that either."

"I'm afraid not," and the actress smiled and shook her head. "We borrowed that from a furrier. Isn't it awful that it's not my own?"

"And the all-lace dress," questioned Miss Cregar dubiously, "where you are sitting by the fireplace in your own parlor serving tea?"

"Oh, that's really mine. I saved for four months to get that dress. You see, that's for when I'm asked out to supper at night. It's fine—I'll show it to you some time."

The faces of the circle brightened considerably.

"But don't you always go out to supper after the play?" came from the outlying chairs.

"No. I'm not always asked—that is, by people I want to go out with—and then, you see, in the profession you've got to rest a lot. You can't very well go out every night and do your work."

349

"Those silk stockings you've got on now," suggested Miss Bowles from her vantage point on the floor, "are awful thin."

Miss Lorelle glanced down at the transparent silk and smiled. "They are thin, aren't they? They're old ones I used to wear on the stage."

Miss Bowles continued. "Do you have to buy your own stockings?"

"Yes, indeed," said Miss Lorelle—"my own stockings and shoes and gloves and—oh, so many things! It's terribly expensive. I don't really know how I'm going to pay my board and the laundry bill sometimes. Managers are not very generous."

"But don't you get a big salary?"

"Pretty big; but then, you see, I have to keep up a show for it. And when my salary goes up, if it ever does, my position will get better, too, and that means that I must use cabs and keep a maid and live in a hotel."

"Do you live in a hotel now?" asked the wide-eyed Miss Wilson.

"Indeed I don't," said the actress. "I'm back in my old room at Miss Burns's, where I lived when I was working here. It's fine to be back again. You remember Miss Burns—she still mothers all the boarders, and the old place is as clean and sweet as it used to be. Just wait until you go on the road, Anna, and live in railroad trains and cheap, stuffy hotels, and you'll be glad to be back in your old home on West Tenth Street, too."

Miss Lorelle glanced at the clock, and rose from her chair. "It's six o'clock, girls," said she, "and you must be getting home. I suppose you still take the six-twenty-six to Rahway, Vera?"

Miss Vera Dobson blushingly admitted that she was still of the great army of commuters. "I know it's a little far," she stammered.

Miss Lorelle put her arms about the girl and kissed her affectionately on the cheek. "I know it is, Vera," she said; "but it's pretty good when you get there— and, after all, it's home, isn't it?"

The girls were moving slowly toward the closets that held their hats and coats. "Oh, Miss Bowles," Miss Lorelle called, "do you have my old desk? I'd so like to see it again." The two girls, arm in arm, moved down the room until they came to the desk where Miss Lorelle had spent so many hours. In a few moments they were joined by the others.

"Must look pretty natural," suggested Miss Cregar—"the books open and the work only half done. You were certainly a pretty bad clerk, Maggie."

Miss Lorelle picked up some of the invoices on the desk and compared them with their numbers in the book. "The same old thing, isn't it?" she said.

"Just the same—there's never any change here. Perhaps you'd like to finish them up for Miss Bowles?"

"Oh, indeed I would," said Miss Lorelle. "Indeed, indeed I would. It would be so like old times. I shouldn't make any mistakes, I promise you."

"It's awfully nice of you," stammered Miss Bowles; "but really——"

"Please let me—just as a favor," and Miss Lorelle held out both her hands. "Good-night, Miss Bowles, and good-night to all of you, girls. I'll stay till Wilson closes up. I want to see him. Old Wilson is still here, isn't he?"

"Yes, he's here all right," said Miss Cregar; "but it don't seem just right to leave you alone, Maggie."

"You always used to leave me alone—you know you did. Run along now, all of you, please."

One by one the seven girls filed before her and wished her good-night, and each one clasped the salmon-pink dress in a fond embrace. When Miss Lorelle was quite alone she sat down in her old chair and turned on the single electric globe above the desk. The shaded light fell full on the books which she had once known so very well. The life of the last year, with all its big troubles and petty successes was forgotten for the moment, and she was back again in the monotonous, happy past of figures and invoices and ledgers. She dipped the pen in the ink and then dropped it back on the desk, just as she used to do, and with her chin resting on her hand she turned toward the open window with its box of fragrant heliotrope and to the quiet little garden of the rectory beyond. She could not have told how long she sat there; but when she heard the door open which led from the private office of the Junior Partner, she hurriedly picked up the pen and began copying the numbers of the invoices in the book before her.

In the dim light Grey did not recognize her, and,

thinking it was one of the clerks, called to her to come into his office.

When he saw Miss Lorelle in the salmon-pink dress standing at the doorway, he hurriedly rose from his desk and received her with much effusion. He had seen her the night before at the Casino, and he, too, had read the stories of the automobiles and the diamonds and the sable coat, and being a young man, apt in the belief of his own world, had placed his own construction upon them.

The girl smiled at the excessive courtesy, and for a brief moment allowed her hand to rest in his. A year before she had left the little room as a discharged employee; now they met on terms of a certain equality —at least of mutual independence.

"This is indeed an honor," said the Junior Partner.

"I came to see the girls," Miss Lorelle replied, glancing at the mass of papers on the desk. "And you—you are still working overtime?" She stood in the centre of the room, looking about her at the portraits and at the other things which had once been so familiar to her.

"Do sit down," urged Grey, "and tell me all about yourself."

Miss Lorelle took the chair in front of the Junior Partner's desk and began slowly pulling on her gloves.

Her late employer leaned against the desk and looked down into the slanting eyes and the oval face shadowed by the big black picture hat.

In that one glance he noted how the change in her life had already written itself in the girl's face—he saw the little lines and the faint shadows. There was an independence too in her manner and an assurance in her speech which he had never known before. In the year past she had acquired a new language.

"It's fine to see you again," he said enthusiastically. "I was at the theatre last night, and was really proud of you. You know I feel, in a way, responsible for your success."

She slowly turned her eyes toward him and then back to the desk. "That—that's what you said to the girl in mauve who sat next to you in the corner of the stage box, wasn't it—I mean at the time I took the first call after my song?"

"Why, yes. I think I did say something of the kind. She really admired you greatly—insisted on asking you to supper with us after the show—and all that sort of thing."

"The lady in mauve must be a very independent young person. And what did you insist on?"

"I? Oh—I was sure that you would have an engagement. I supposed you would be celebrating your success at Rector's; in fact, I dropped in there late in the hope of seeing you; but you weren't there, were you?"

"No, I wasn't there—nobody happened to ask me to supper last night; so I went alone to Mr. Mink's. Perhaps you don't know Mr. Mink's—it's a rather clean little place over on Sixth avenue— and you sit on a high stool, and the food is piled all around you on glass-covered stands."

"Really?" said the Junior Partner. He looked down curiously at the girl, who had taken up his pen and was beating a slow tattoo with it on the desk blotter. "One often gets such wrong ideas," he added. "I thought, of course, that you would be with your friends."

"I'm afraid I have no friends in New York except the girls in the office here, and their interest appeared to fade a bit when they heard that my automobile and my jewels were only pipe dreams of the press agent. They seemed glad enough to go home at six o'clock when I told them I still used the street cars. But they're all right—after all, it's pretty good to have a home to go to."

"But I can't imagine all those girls' homes are so attractive as that," interrupted the Junior Partner.

"No, you can't imagine and they can't imagine what the same four walls and the same faces and the same little welcome means every evening at the same hour. I know it's monotonous enough, all right; but I'll tell you what it stands for to a girl—it stands for a kind of protection. If a wise guy of an hotel clerk with a grin on his face gave you a key to a new home every night, or at most once a week, that same monotony would get to seem pretty good." The girl tossed the pen on the desk and looked squarely into the face of the Junior Partner.

"Do you know the best hour of the day to me—now?"

Grey shook his head, and slowly folded his arms.

"I'll tell you—it's six o'clock—when the whistles blow; because wherever I am, whatever city or any old one-night stand I happen to be in, I know that all over the town there are hundreds of men and women shutting down their desks and putting on their hats and going home—home. When they're at work, I'm either in a room in a raw hotel or walking the main street and being pointed out as one of 'the troupe'; and when night comes around I am at work with paint on my face trying to amuse these same people. And I'll tell you, Mr. Grey, even if a girl does succeed in this business, these same hours go for the woman star as well as for the girl in the back row; and the next time you see your lady friend in the mauve dress you might tell her all this, too. It will take longer to say than that you put me in the business; but it's just as true, and it will make conversation."

Miss Lorelle rose from her seat at the desk, and, crossing the room, stopped in front of the looking-glass over the fireplace and carefully adjusted her hat. Reflected in the mirror, she saw the good-looking features of Grey smiling quizzically at her from across the room.

"And oh, Mr. Grey," she said, patting her hair at the temples and smiling at the reflection in the glass, "do thank the lady in mauve for wanting me to come to supper. It does seem queer that the man who wouldn't ask me was the same one that lifted me out of the clerking game and that put me in the show business." She turned and held out her hand to him. "Good-by, Mr. Grey—I'm going outside to wait for Wilson. I want to see him when he makes his round."

The Junior Partner took her hand in both of his. "I'm sorry," he said—"very, very sorry if I made a mistake. I'm sure you will admit that I meant well."

"Meant well? Why, of course, you meant well!" With her free hand the girl carefully brushed a speck from the lapel of the coat of the Junior Partner. "But say, honest for fair, don't you find that most of the trouble in this world comes from the people who mean well—I mean the self-appointed understudies for the general manager of the universe? And now if you'll kindly let me have that hand back, which I need in my business, I'll say good-by."

And with these words the pale, smiling face and the salmon-pink dress of Miss Lorelle passed forever out of the social life of the Junior Partner.